SCREENO:

STORIES & POEMS

DELMORE SCHWARTZ

SCREENO:
STORIES & POEMS

Introduction by CYNTHIA OZICK

A NEW DIRECTIONS
Bibelot

PUBLISHER'S NOTE: New Directions wishes to thank Robert Phillips. With Rob
House, he made the selection in Screeno: Stories & Poems and served as wise friend
and consultant.

For a selection from "Gerontion" in Collected Poems by T. S. Eliot (copyright 1936 by
Harcourt Brace Jovanovich, Inc.; copyright © 1963, 1964 by T. S. Eliot), reprinted
by permission of Harcourt Brace Jovanovich, Inc., and Faber and Faber Ltd.

Manufactured in the United States of America
New Directions Books are printed on acid-free paper.
First published as a New Directions Bibelot (NDP 985) in 2004
Published simultaneously in Canada by Penguin Books Canada Limited

Cover design by Semadar Megged; interior design by Arlene Goldberg.

Library of Congress Cataloging-in-Publication Data

Schwartz, Delmore, 1913-1966.
Screeno : stories & poems / Delmore Schwartz; introduction by Cynthia Ozick.
    p. cm. — (New Directions paperbook ; 985)
ISBN 0-8112-1573-3 (alk. paper)
I. Title.
PS3537.C79A6 2004
818'.52—dc22   2004004050

New Directions Books are published for James Laughlin
by New Directions Publishing Corporation,
80 Eighth Avenue, New York 10011

Table of Contents

Introduction

CYNTHIA OZICK

Like Sylvia Plath a generation later, like Shelley a century before, Delmore Schwartz is one of those poets whose life inescapably rivals the work. Plath's fame is linked as much to the shock of the suicide as to the shock of the poetry; the wild romance of Shelley's lines is fulfilled in the drama of the drowning. And Delmore Schwartz catapults past the fickleness of mere reputation (that posture and position which Lionel Trilling defined as characterizing a "figure") into something close to legend. What puts him there is not his ignominious end—he died, at fifty-three, after living in chaotic solitude in a Manhattan hotel—but the clamorous periods of derangement that rocked him, side by side with spurts of virtuosity. It was a catastrophic life—turbulent, demanding, importuning, drinking, pill-swallowing, competitive, suspicious, litigious. He reveled in celebrity when it came to him and abused the friendships it attracted. At one point he appeared ready to sue nearly every literary luminary he knew. His incessant talk turned to aggressive harangue and accusation. But he early saw into the logic of his madness, attributing it to the rage of an ambition too overreaching ever to be attained. "The torment of disappointed hope becomes a brutality to myself," he wrote.

He was, like many of the so-called New York Intellectuals of his generation, the aspiring son of Jewish immigrants. His parents were mismatched; his philandering father prospered in real estate until the Crash. Delmore followed sports, went obsessively to the movies, and judged his family and broken household with a harshly dismissive yet hotly bonded eye. As an undergraduate at the University of Wisconsin, he fell deliriously into modernism, Eliot and Pound and Joyce, and was steeped in avant-garde periodicals like *Hound & Horn*—but he failed Latin, and except for English made an indifferent record. He returned to New York to study philosophy with Sidney Hook and James Burnham at NYU's Washington Square College, where he met the first of his two wives. Both eventually left him; upheaval and rancor trailed him all his fabled days.

Philosophy next lured him to Harvard. He worked at it under the eminent Alfred North Whitehead, but at length began to waver, and poetry won out. Yet philosophy infiltrated the poetry—not through narrow cognitive distinctions, but through discerning the naked *there*ness of things. Philosophy gave his lines the crystalline quality of naiveté: the peculiar power to gaze into the self, or the world, as objects never before seen or contemplated. He became a metaphysician of the near-at-hand:

> If you look long enough at anything
> It will become extremely interesting;
> If you look very long at anything
> It will become rich, manifold, fascinating.

Out of Whitehead's "the withness of the body" came

> The heavy bear who goes with me,
> A manifold honey to smear his face,
> Clumsy and lumbering here and there,

8

The central ton of every place

. . .

That inescapable animal that walks with me,
Has followed me since the black womb held,
Moves where I move, distorting my gesture,
A caricature, a swollen shadow,
A stupid clown of the spirit's motive,
Perplexes and affronts with his own darkness,
The secret life of belly and bone,
Opaque, too near, my private, yet unknown . . .

The penetration of this opacity Schwartz called "the parsing of context." His own body was a context to be parsed, however mercilessly, and even his name, the lyrical Delmore, was an outerness hinting at inner life: on the principle of *nomen est numen*—name is spirit—only a poet could be destined for so poetic a name. But such parsing will not inevitably lead to self-understanding. In "March 29" he cries:

Behold! For we are absent from our knowledge,we are lost to the common undertaking of our lives, there are unleashed within us the small animals of silence. . . .

And in the shimmeringly titled "In the Naked Bed, in Plato's Cave" an alert heaping-up of the poet's surround accretes—aural, visual, atmospheric, above all needlingly concrete: the window and the window curtains, trucks passing, the milkman's footsteps, the bottles' clink, the horse, the street, the streetlight, the sky, a car's starter, a chair, a mirror, a dresser, a wall, a birdcall! Though each of these is possessed by an explicit *presence*, taken together all fall into elusive enigma:

                                      Perplexed, still wet
            With sleep, affectionate, hungry and cold.
                                                  So, so,
            O son of man, the ignorant night, the travail
            Of early morning, the mystery of beginning
            Again and again,
                                        while History is unforgiven.

   From the bedroom and its furnishings, to the mun-
dane city-sounds of early morning, to the heartless chron-
icle of humankind.
   Why is history unforgiven? Perhaps because it is,
after all, history, out of which all contradictions can be
wrested and made palpable. "I hate an abstract thing," he
complains in "The Ballad of the Children of the Czar"—
wherein the Czar's children bounce a ball in the Czar's
garden, while that same year Delmore, "aged two, irrational," eats a baked potato in Brooklyn, "six thousand
miles apart." The Czar's children play among flowerbeds,
but the poet recalls that his grandfather, coughing and
wretched in the Czar's army, flees to America, "to
become," he notes sardonically, "a king himself." The
bouncing ball among the flowers and the baked potato
in Brooklyn swell hugely, balefully, transmuted finally
into the round earth itself, the "wheeling, whirling
world":

            A pitiless, purposeless Thing,
            Arbitrary and unspent

                          . . .

            I am overtaken by terror
            Thinking of my father's fathers,
            And of my own will.

                              10

The innocently small, the innocently tangible can shockingly lurch into widening empty blind unknowingness: so that elsewhere, a night train with its passengers, the smoke, the dark, the "pencil lines of telephone posts, crucified," the scenes that rush by, turning away from hope, from history itself, reveal only "the overnight endless trip to the famous unfathomable abyss":

> O your life, your lonely life
> What have you done with it,
> And done with the great gift of consciousness?

Writing of Baudelaire, and purporting to enact the French poet's recklessly desperate psyche, it is himself whom Schwartz uncovers:

> I am sick of this life of furnished rooms.
> I am sick of having colds and headaches:
> You know my strange life. Every day brings
>
> Its quota of wrath. You little know
> A poet's life, dear Mother: I must write
>   poems,
> The most fatiguing of occupations.

Though intimations of the then prevailing imperium of *The Waste Land* seep through many of Schwartz's verses, and though they are permeated by the sort of acutely objective self-consciousness that characterizes much of the modernist ethos, Schwartz cannot, either in his poetry or his prose, be wholly defined as a modernist—a judgment that might have alarmed him. The tenor of his mind is largely like the tenor of his extravagantly Romantic given name—Romantically excessive, even incongruous, especially in the company of workaday Schwartz. Allusions, nineteenth-century-style, to Dionysus and Venus, to "Attic dust," "love's victory," "the day's splendor," "lights' glory," "his smile which glows like that of the spring moon," "the miracle of love," and abundantly more in that vein, attest more to Keats than to Prufrock, and more to earnest odes to beauty and despair than to anxious dead-pan skeptical modernist reticence. "Everywhere radiance glows like a garden in stillness blossoming" is an idiom that, in all its shameless loveliness, seizes on the old roots of poetry. And here, in "Seurat's Sunday Afternoon along the Seine," one can catch, with rapt directness, the uncon-cealed Keatsian tone:

> O happy, happy throng,
> It is forever Sunday, summer, free

All this discloses a poet's escape, if he wills it, from the commanding *Zeitgeist*. Or even if he does not will it, if it comes unwittingly, unsummoned, from his nature—libertarian, untethered, deaf to all authority but the imperative inward chant. How else account for the star-tling grandeur of "Starlight Like Intuition Pierced the Twelve," a title that, even apart from the lines that follow, carries a nimbus almost too bright to bear?

Put it that the poetry is Delmore; its themes are chiefly (and in his own fearsome words), *awe* and *abyss*. But the prose? The prose is Schwartz. The language of the stories is plain, simple, never convoluted or mandarin; practical and ordinary. "It is Sunday afternoon, June 12th, 1909, and my father is on his way to visit my mother," commences the second paragraph of "In Dreams Begin Responsibilities," Schwartz's most celebrated fiction. No Seurat's Sunday afternoon here; no happy throngs. The narrator sits in a darkened movie house in the days of silent film, witnessing the unfolding courtship of his parents. "The shots themselves," he explains, "are full of dots and rays, as if it were raining when the picture was photographed. The light is bad." And in the narrative itself there are few rays and many dots: the sentences are short and declarative:

> As my father enters, my grandfather rises from the table and shakes hands with him. My mother has run upstairs to tidy herself. My grandmother asks my father if he has had dinner, and tells him that Rose will be downstairs soon. My grandfather opens the conversation by remarking on the mild June weather. My father sits uncomfortably near the table, holding his hat in his hand. My grandmother tells my aunt to take my father's hat.

These flat, even commonplace, cadences—as flat and commonplace as the name Schwartz—appear to have no affinity with the baroque Delmorean movements of the poems. Did the same mind coin them? At first sight, hardly; the gap between verse and fiction seems antagonistic, nearly schizophrenic: on the one hand wild eloquence (the wine-pitcher broken and spilling), while on the other subdued dry orderliness. Yet the stories have a labyrinthine undersea quality; cumulatively, the pedestrian turns tragic and surreal. As the narrator sees his father proposing marriage to his mother on the movie screen, he leaps out of his seat and shouts, "Don't do it. It's not too late to change your minds, both of you. Nothing good will come of it, only remorse, hatred, scandal, and two children whose characters are monstrous." What has begun prosaically becomes hideously visionary: the Delmorean abyss again opening, ready to swallow the dreamer; the dreamer's prefigured and ineluctable birth

13

dreaded and doomed. It is a terrifying tale of the willed abortion of the self.

Movies—the dream palaces of the thirties and forties—dominate other fictions. "Screeno" recalls a period when theaters featured on-stage allurements in addition to the picture, often in the form of lotteries offering money prizes. Cornelius Schmidt, a lonely and impoverished self-declared young poet, wins at Screeno, at first resenting and then championing a usurping rival for the prize. The story pivots on the shiftings of perception and reality, on the longings of youth and the lamentations of age; and on uncanny Kafkan reversals. Here and there philosophy peers in: "'Oh,' said Cornelius to himself, 'they are going to start the whole objective and subjective business again'"—until it is finally clear that this story, too, owes more to the shadows of dreams than to local movie-house history. The movie-goer with the winning ticket is gambling for control of his slippery life—below which, as always, gapes the abyss.

A third movie story concerns Hugo Bauer, a rich financier who lusts after a Hollywood screen goddess, whom he ultimately marries. Divorce quickly follows. But it is her naked image he has fallen in love with, the seductive phantom projected in her notorious film, "The Heights of Joy." To possess this image wholly for himself, he attempts to buy and destroy all existing copies of it, "devoting himself to a senseless quest in which his life became just as bewitched and monomaniacal, as passionate and as narrow, as the life of a gambler or a lyric poet." Despite every effort, the film cannot be sequestered from other eyes, since new copies can repeatedly be made; but years later, when the marriage is long forgotten, the image of Hugo Bauer's former wife, "naked and radiant as the moonlight on a midsummer night, shining and distant and unattainable," unreels before him, and he is exalted.

14

The stories are all of a piece. They are shrewd Schwartzian tricksters that may momentarily fool you into thinking you have been kidnapped into the land of the declarative sentence; but this is sleight-of-hand. In the end the stories are seen to be, bone for bone, blood for blood, of the same Delmorean germ plasm as the poems. A case in point is "The Statues," a vision in which a strange snow falls, assuming permanent forms that will not melt or give way.

> Many of these statues were grotesque. Some were monstrous. Some resembled human figures, and although they were of a perfect verisimilitude in all else, the faces were at times blank as a plate, distorted like gargoyles, or obscene, as when, in certain suburbs, figures clung to each other in an embrace which was hardly ambiguous. Elsewhere, however, the statues had the rotundity and the plumpness of the cumulus clouds of a summer's day, the solidity and the stillness of fine buildings, or the pure and easy design of some flowers. Everywhere were forms which delighted the eye either as fresh complexes of previously known designs, or compositions which seemed to exhaust the possibility of arrangement.

The stories, like many of the poems, are dreams without responsibilities. They are their own cause, their own authority, their own unreasoning reason.

* * *

Delmore Schwartz, some dare to say, is in eclipse. With the acceleration of the generations, his fame is long dimmed; the *Wunderkind* he once was is unremembered.

15

His life—that tumultuous unstoppable speechifying, the madness that tossed and tormented and ruined him—stands like one of those impermeable statues of his imagining. Saul Bellow, in snatching Delmore's persona for *Humboldt's Gift*, knowingly wrote his epitaph:

> For after all Humboldt did what poets in crass America are supposed to do. He chased ruin and death even harder than he had chased women. He blew his talent and his health and reached home, the grave, in a dusty slide. He plowed himself under. . . . Such was the attitude reflected in the picture of Humboldt the *Times* chose to use. It was one of those mad-rotten-majesty pictures—spooky, humorless, glaring furiously with tight lips, mumpish or scrofulous cheeks, a scarred forehead, and a look of enraged, ravaged childishness. This was the Humboldt of conspiracies, putsches, accusations, tantrums, the Bellevue Hospital Humboldt. . . .

But a poet all the same. He plowed himself under? Never mind. Delmore Schwartz in death casts off the heavy bear, leaving behind awe and abyss, dream and chant.

SCREENO:

Stories & Poems

In the Naked Bed, in Plato's Cave

In the naked bed, in Plato's cave,
Reflected headlights slowly slid the wall,
Carpenters hammered under the shaded window,
Wind troubled the window curtains all night long,
A fleet of trucks strained uphill, grinding,
Their freights covered, as usual.
The ceiling lightened again, the slanting diagram
Slid slowly forth.
                    Hearing the milkman's chop,
His striving up the stair, the bottle's chink,
I rose from bed, lit a cigarette,
And walked to the window. The stony street
Displayed the stillness in which buildings stand,
The street-lamp's vigil and the horse's patience.
The winter sky's pure capital
Turned me back to bed with exhausted eyes.

Strangeness grew in the motionless air. The loose
Film grayed. Shaking wagons, hooves' waterfalls,
Sounded far off, increasing, louder and nearer.
A car coughed, starting. Morning, softly
Melting the air, lifted the half-covered chair
From underseas, kindled the looking-glass,
Distinguished the dresser and the white wall.
The bird called tentatively, whistled, called,
Bubbled and whistled, so! Perplexed, still wet
With sleep, affectionate, hungry and cold. So, so,
O son of man, the ignorant night, the travail

Of early morning, the mystery of beginning
Again and again,
while History is unforgiven.

The Ballet of the Fifth Year

Where the sea gulls sleep or indeed where they fly
Is a place of different traffic. Although I
Consider the fishing bay (where I see them dip and curve
And purely glide) a place that weakens the nerve
Of will, and closes my eyes, as they should not be
(They should burn like the street-light all night quietly,
So that whatever is present will be known to me),
Nevertheless the gulls and the imagination
Of where they sleep, which comes to creation
In strict shape and color, from their dallying
Their wings slowly, and suddenly rallying
Over, up, down the arabesque of descent,
Is an old act enacted, my fabulous intent
When I skated, afraid of policemen, five years old,
In the winter sunset, sorrowful and cold,
Hardly attained to thought, but old enough to know
Such grace, so self-contained, was the best escape to know.

The Beautiful American Word, Sure

The beautiful American word, Sure,
As I have come into a room, and touch
The lamp's button, and the light blooms with such
Certainty where the darkness loomed before,

As I care for what I do not know, and care
Knowing for little she might not have been,
And for how little she would be unseen,
The intercourse of lives miraculous and dear.

Where the light is, and each thing clear,
Separate from all others, standing in its place,
I drink the time and touch whatever's near,

And hope for day when the whole world has that face:
For what assures her present every year?
In dark accidents the mind's sufficient grace.

March 29

"The man looked up as the sun went down
                              and I thought
Brother,
behold the parsing of our context, the wind
shrinks from the felicity of the light, the infant
Dionysus springing from Apollo's arm, and
Hermes' nose, the lips of Cupid, the eyes
the black eyes of Venus' sister,
Split, furrowed, creased, mottled, stained
secret—Behold! For we are absent from our knowledge,
                                                    we are
lost to the common undertaking of our lives, there are
unleashed within us the small animals of silence,
and these keep watch between us.—neither my brother
nor I nor the brown air which protected us
will ever give heed the one to the other!"

Will You Perhaps Consent To Be
"méntre il vento, come fa, si tace"

Will you perhaps consent to be
Now that a little while is still
(Ruth of sweet wind) now that a little while
My mind's continuing and unreleasing wind
Touches this single of your flowers, this one only,
Will you perhaps consent to be
My many-branched, small and dearest tree?

My mind's continuing and unreleasing wind
—The wind which is wild and restless, tired and asleep,
The wind which is tired, wild and still continuing,
The wind which is chill, and warm, wet, soft, in every
                                                    influence,
Lusts for Paris, Crete and Pergamus,
Is suddenly off for Paris and Chicago,
Judaea, San Francisco, the Midi
—May I perhaps return to you
Wet with an Attic dust and chill from Norway
My dear, so-many-branched smallest tree?

Would you perhaps consent to be
The very rack and crucifix of winter, winter's wild
Knife-edged, continuing and unreleasing,
Intent and stripping, ice-caressing wind?
My dear, most dear, so-many-branched tree
My mind's continuing and unreleasing wind
Touches this single of your flowers, faith in me,
Wide as the—sky!—accepting as the (air)!
—Consent, consent, consent to be
My many-branched, small and dearest tree.

22

What Is To Be Given

What is to be given,
Is spirit, yet animal,
Colored, like heaven,
Blue, yellow, beautiful.

The blood is checkered by
So many stains and wishes,
Between it and the sky
You could not choose, for riches.

Yet let me now be careful
Not to give too much
To one so shy and fearful
For like a gun is touch.

The Ballad of the Children of the Czar

1

The children of the Czar
Played with a bouncing ball

In the May morning, in the Czar's garden,
Tossing it back and forth.

It fell among the flowerbeds
Or fled to the north gate.

A daylight moon hung up
In the Western sky, bald white.

Like Papa's face, said Sister,
Hurling the white ball forth.

2

While I ate a baked potato
Six thousand miles apart,

In Brooklyn, in 1916,
Aged two, irrational.

When Franklin D. Roosevelt
Was an Arrow Collar ad.

O Nicholas! Alas! Alas!
My grandfather coughed in your army,

Hid in a wine-stinking barrel,
For three days in Bucharest

Then left for America
To become a king himself.

3

I am my father's father,
You are your children's guilt.

In history's pity and terror
The child is Aeneas again;

Troy is in the nursery,
The rocking horse is on fire.

Child labor! The child must carry
His fathers on his back.

But seeing that so much is past
And that history has no ruth

For the individual,
Who drinks tea, who catches cold,

Let anger be general:
I hate an abstract thing.

4

Brother and sister bounced
The bounding, unbroken ball,

The shattering sun fell down
Like swords upon their play,

Moving eastward among the stars
Toward February and October.

But the Maywind brushed their cheeks
Like a mother watching sleep,

And if for a moment they fight
Over the bouncing ball

And sister pinches brother
And brother kicks her shins,

Well! The heart of man is known:
It is a cactus bloom.

5

The ground on which the ball bounces
Is another bouncing ball.

The wheeling, whirling world
Makes no will glad.

Spinning in its spotlight darkness,
It is too big for their hands.

A pitiless, purposeless Thing,
Arbitrary and unspent,

Made for no play, for no children,
But chasing only itself.
The innocent are overtaken,
They are not innocent.

They are their father's fathers,
The past is inevitable.

6

Now, in another October
Of this tragic star,

I see my second year,
I eat my baked potato.

It is my buttered world,
But, poked by my unlearned hand,

It falls from the highchair down
And I begin to howl.

And I see the ball roll under
The iron gate which is locked.

Sister is screaming, brother is howling,
The ball has evaded their will.

Even a bouncing ball
Is uncontrollable,

And is under the garden wall.
I am overtaken by terror

Thinking of my father's fathers,
And of my own will.

What Curious Dresses All Men Wear

What curious dresses all men wear!
The walker you met in a brown study,
The President smug in rotogravure,
The mannequin, the bathing beauty.

The bubble-dancer, the deep-sea diver,
The bureaucrat, the adulterer,
Hide private parts which I disclose
To those who know what a poem knows.

Baudelaire

When I fall asleep, and even during sleep,
I hear, quite distinctly, voices speaking

Whole phrases, commonplace and trivial,
Having no relation to my affairs.

Dear Mother, is any time left to us
In which to be happy? My debts are immense.
My bank account is subject to the court's judgment.
I know nothing. I cannot know anything.
I have lost the ability to make an effort.
But now as before my love for you increases.
You are always armed to stone me, always:
It is true. It dates from childhood.

For the first time in my long life
I am almost happy. The book, almost finished,
Almost seems good. It will endure, a monument
To my obsessions, my hatred, my disgust.

Debts and inquietude persist and weaken me.
Satan glides before me, saying sweetly:
"Rest for a day! You can rest and play today.
Tonight you will work." When night comes,
My mind, terrified by the arrears,
Bored by sadness, paralyzed by impotence,
Promises: 'Tomorrow: I will tomorrow.'"
Tomorrow the same comedy enacts itself
With the same resolution, the same weakness.
I am sick of this life of furnished rooms.
I am sick of having colds and headaches:
You know my strange life. Every day brings

Its quota of wrath. You little know
A poet's life, dear Mother: I must write poems,
The most fatiguing of occupations.

I am sad this morning. Do not reproach me.

I write from a café near the post office,
Amid the click of billiard balls, the clatter of dishes,
The pounding of my heart. I have been asked to write
"A History of Caricature." I have been asked to write
"A History of Sculpture." Shall I write a history
Of the caricatures of the sculptures of you in my heart?

Although it costs you countless agony,
Although you cannot believe it necessary,
And doubt that the sum is accurate,
Please send me money enough for at least three weeks.

All Night, All Night

I have been one acquainted with the night
—ROBERT FROST

Rode in the train all night, in the sick light. A bird
Flew parallel with a singular will. In daydream's moods and
attitudes
The other passengers slumped, dozed, slept, read,
Waiting, and waiting for place to be displaced
On the exact track of safety or the rack of accident.

Looked out at the night, unable to distinguish
Lights in the towns of passage from the yellow lights
Numb on the ceiling. And the bird flew parallel and still
As the train shot forth the straight line of its whistle,
Forward on the taut tracks, piercing empty, familiar—

The bored center of this vision and condition looked and
looked
Down through the slick pages of the magazine (seeking

The seen and the unseen) and his gaze fell down the well.
Of the great darkness under the slick glitter,
And he was only one among eight million riders and
                                                readers.
And all the while under his empty smile the shaking drum
Of the long determined passage passed through him
By his body mimicked and echoed. And then the train,
Like a suddenly storming rain, began to rush and thresh
The silent or passive night, pressing and impressing
The patients' foreheads with a tightening-like image
Of the rushing engine proceeded by a shaft of light
Piercing the dark, changing and transforming the silence
Into a violence of foam, sound, smoke and succession.

A bored child went to get a cup of water,
And crushed the cup because the water too was
Boring and merely boredom's struggle.
The child, returning, looked over the shoulder
Of a man reading until he annoyed the shoulder.
A fat woman yawned and felt the liquid drops
Drip down the fleece of many dinners.

And the bird flew parallel and parallel flew
The black pencil lines of telephone posts, crucified,
At regular intervals, post after post
Of thrice crossed, blue-belled, anonymous trees.

And then the bird cried as if to all of us:

> *O your life, your lonely life*
> *What have you ever done with it.*
> *And done with the great gift of consciousness?*
> *What will you ever do with your life before*
> *   death's knife*

As I for my part felt in my heart as one who falls,
Falls in a parachute, falls endlessly, and feel the vast
Draft of the abyss sucking him down and down,
An endlessly helplessly falling and appalled clown:

This is the way that night passes by, this
Is the overnight endless trip to the famous unfathomable
abyss.

A Dog Named Ego,
the Snowflakes as Kisses

A dog named Ego, the snowflakes as kisses
Fluttered, ran, came with me in December,
Snuffing the chill air, changing, and halting,
There where I walked toward seven o'clock,
Sniffed at some interests hidden and open,
Whirled, descending, and stood still, attentive
Seeking their peace, the stranger, unknown,
With me, near me, kissed me, touched my wound,
My simple face, obsessed and pleasure bound.

"Not free, no liberty, rock that you carry,"
So spoke Ego in his cracked and harsh voice,
While snowflakes kissed me and satisfied minutes,
Falling from some place half believed and unknown,
"You will not be free, nor ever alone,"
So spoke Ego, "Mine is the kingdom,
Dynasty's bone: you will not be free,
Go, choose, run, you will not be alone."

"Come, come, come," sang the whirling snowflakes,
Evading the dog who barked at their smallness,
"Come!" sang the snowflakes, "Come here! and here!"
How soon at the sidewalk, melted, and done,
One kissed me, two kissed me! So many died!
While Ego barked at them, swallowed their touch,
Ran this way! And that way! While they slipped to the
                                                    ground,

Leading him further and farther away,
While night collapsed amid the falling,
And left me no recourse, far from my home,
And left me no recourse, far from my home.

America, America!

I am a poet of the Hudson River and the heights above it,
            the lights, the stars, and the bridges
I am also by self-appointment the laureate of the Atlantic
            —of the peoples' hearts, crossing it
                to new America.

I am burdened with the truck and chimera, hope,
            acquired in the sweating sick-excited passage
                    in steerage, strange and estranged
Hence I must descry and describe the kingdom of emotion.

For I am a poet of the kindergarten (in the city)
            and the cemetery (in the city)
And rapture and ragtime and also the secret city in the
                                            heart and mind
This is the song of the natural city self in the 20th century.

It is true but only partly true that a city is a "tyranny of
                                                    numbers"
(This is the chant of the urban metropolitan and
                                        metaphysical self
After the first two World Wars of the 20th century)

—This is the city self, looking from window to
                                    lighted window
When the squares and checks of faintly yellow light
Shine at night, upon a huge dim board and slab-like tombs,
Hiding many lives. It is the city consciousness
Which sees and says: more: more and more: always more.

Poem

In the morning, when it was raining,
Then the birds were hectic and loudy;
Through all the reign is fall's entertaining;
Their singing was erratic and full of disorder:
They did not remember the summer blue
Or the orange of June. They did not think at all
Of the great red and bursting ball
Of the kingly sun's terror and tempest, blazing,
Once the slanting rain threw over all
The colorless curtains of the ceaseless spontaneous fall.

In Dreams Begin Responsibilities

I

I think it is the year 1909. I feel as if I were in a motion picture theatre, the long arm of light crossing the darkness and spinning, my eyes fixed on the screen. This is a silent picture as if an old Biograph one, in which the actors are dressed in ridiculously old-fashioned clothes, and one flash succeeds another with sudden jumps. The actors too seem to jump about and walk too fast. The shots themselves are full of dots and rays, as if it were raining when the picture was photographed. The light is bad.

It is Sunday afternoon, June 12th, 1909, and my father is walking down the quiet streets of Brooklyn on his way to visit my mother. His clothes are newly pressed and his tie is too tight in his high collar. He jingles the coins in his pockets, thinking of the witty things he will say. I feel as if I had by now relaxed entirely in the soft darkness of the theatre; the organist peals out the obvious and approximate emotions on which the audience rocks unknowingly. I am anonymous, and I have forgotten myself. It is always so when one goes to the movies, it is, as they say, a drug.

My father walks from street to street of trees, lawns and houses, once in a while coming to an avenue on which a streetcar skates and gnaws, slowly progressing. The conductor, who has a handle-bar mustache, helps a young lady wearing a hat like a bowl with feathers on to the car. She lifts her long skirts slightly as she mounts the steps. He leisurely makes change and rings his bell. It is obviously Sunday, for everyone is wearing Sunday clothes, and the street-car's noises emphasize the quiet of the holiday. Is not Brooklyn the City of Churches? The shops are closed and their shades drawn, but for an occasional stationery store or drug-store with great green balls in the window.

My father has chosen to take this long walk because he likes to walk and think. He thinks about himself in the future and so arrives at the place he is to visit in a state of mild exaltation. He pays no attention to the houses he is passing, in which the Sunday dinner is being eaten, nor to the many trees which patrol each street, now coming to their full leafage and the time when they will room the whole street in cool shadow. An occasional carriage passes, the horse's hooves falling like stones in the quiet afternoon, and once in a while an automobile, looking like an enormous upholstered sofa, puffs and passes.

My father thinks of my mother, of how nice it will be to introduce her to his family. But he is not yet sure that he wants to marry her, and once in a while he becomes panicky about the bond already established. He reassures himself by thinking of the big men he admires who are married: William Randolph Hearst, and William Howard Taft, who has just become President of the United States.

My father arrives at my mother's house. He has come too early and so is suddenly embarrassed. My aunt, my mother's sister, answers the loud bell with her napkin in her hand, for the family is still at dinner. As my father enters, my grandfather rises from the table and shakes hands with him. My mother has run upstairs to tidy herself. My grandmother asks my father if he has had dinner, and tells him that Rose will be downstairs soon. My grandfather opens the conversation by remarking on the mild June weather. My father sits uncomfortably near the table, holding his hat in his hand. My grandmother tells my aunt to take my father's hat. My uncle, twelve years old, runs into the house, his hair tousled. He shouts a

35

greeting to my father, who has often given him a nickel, and then runs upstairs. It is evident that the respect in which my father is held in this household is tempered by a good deal of mirth. He is impressive, yet he is very awkward.

II

Finally my mother comes downstairs, all dressed up, and my father being engaged in conversation with my grandfather becomes uneasy, not knowing whether to greet my mother or continue the conversation. He gets up from the chair clumsily and says "hello" gruffly. My grandfather watches, examining their congruence, such as it is, with a critical eye, and meanwhile rubbing his bearded cheek roughly, as he always does when he reflects. He is worried; he is afraid that my father will not make a good husband for his oldest daughter. At this point something happens to the film, just as my father is saying something funny to my mother; I am awakened to myself and my unhappiness just as my interest was rising. The audience begins to clap impatiently. Then the trouble is cared for but the film has been returned to a portion just shown, and once more I see my grandfather rubbing his bearded cheek and pondering my father's character. It is difficult to get back into the picture once more and forget myself, but as my mother giggles at my father's words, the darkness drowns me.

My father and mother depart from the house, my father shaking hands with my mother once more, out of some unknown uneasiness. I stir uneasily also, slouched in the hard chair of the theatre. Where is the older uncle, my mother's older brother? He is studying in his bedroom upstairs, studying for his final examination at the College of the City of New York, having been dead of rapid pneu-

36

monia for the last twenty-one years. My mother and father walk down the same quiet streets once more. My mother is holding my father's arm and telling him of the novel which she has been reading; and my father utters judgments of the characters as the plot is made clear to him. This is a habit which he very much enjoys, for he feels the utmost superiority and confidence when he approves and condemns the behavior of other people. At times he feels moved to utter a brief "Ugh"—whenever the story becomes what he would call sugary. This tribute is paid to his manliness. My mother feels satisfied by the interest which she has awakened; she is showing my father how intelligent she is, and how interesting.

They reach the avenue, and the street-car leisurely arrives. They are going to Coney Island this afternoon, although my mother considers that such pleasures are inferior. She has made up her mind to indulge only in a walk on the boardwalk and a pleasant dinner, avoiding the riotous amusements as being beneath the dignity of so dignified a couple.

My father tells my mother how much money he has made in the past week, exaggerating an amount which need not have been exaggerated. But my father has always felt that actualities somehow fall short. Suddenly I begin to weep. The determined old lady who sits next to me in the theatre is annoyed and looks at me with an angry face, and being intimidated, I stop. I drag out my handkerchief and dry my face, licking the drop which has fallen near my lips. Meanwhile I have missed something, for here are my mother and father alighting at the last stop, Coney Island.

III

They walk toward the boardwalk, and my father commands my mother to inhale the pungent air from the sea. They both breathe in deeply, both of them laughing as they do so. They have in common a great interest in health, although my father is strong and husky, my mother frail. Their minds are full of theories of what is good to eat and not good to eat, and sometimes they engage in heated discussions of the subject, the whole matter ending in my father's announcement, made with a scornful bluster, that you have to die sooner or later anyway. On the boardwalk's flagpole, the American flag is pulsing in an intermittent wind from the sea.

My father and mother go to the rail of the boardwalk and look down on the beach where a good many bathers are casually walking about. A few are in the surf. A peanut whistle pierces the air with its pleasant and active whine, and my father goes to buy peanuts. My mother remains at the rail and stares at the ocean. The ocean seems merry to her; it pointedly sparkles and again and again the pony waves are released. She notices the children digging in the wet sand, and the bathing costumes of the girls who are her own age. My father returns with the peanuts. Overhead the sun's lightning strikes and strikes, but neither of them are at all aware of it. The boardwalk is full of people dressed in their Sunday clothes and idly strolling. The tide does not reach as far as the boardwalk, and the strollers would feel no danger if it did. My mother and father lean on the rail of the boardwalk and absently stare at the ocean. The ocean is becoming rough; the waves come in slowly, tugging strength from far back. The moment before they somersault, the moment when they arch their backs so beautifully, showing green and white veins amid the black, that moment is intolerable. They finally crack, dashing

38

fiercely upon the sand, actually driving, full force downward, against the sand, bouncing upward and forward, and at last petering out into a small stream which races up the beach and then is recalled. My parents gaze absentmindedly at the ocean, scarcely interested in its harshness. The sun overhead does not disturb them. But I stare at the terrible sun which breaks up sight, and the fatal, merciless, passionate ocean, I forget my parents. I stare fascinated and finally, shocked by the indifference of my father and mother, I burst out weeping once more. The old lady next to me pats me on the shoulder and says "There, there, all of this is only a movie, young man, only a movie," but I look up once more at the terrifying sun and the terrifying ocean, and being unable to control my tears, I get up and go to the men's room, stumbling over the feet of the other people seated in my row.

IV

When I return, feeling as if I had awakened in the morning sick for lack of sleep, several hours have apparently passed and my parents are riding on the merry-go-round. My father is on a black horse, my mother on a white one, and they seem to be making an eternal circuit for the single purpose of snatching the nickel rings which are attached to the arm of one of the posts. A hand-organ is playing; it is one with the ceaseless circling of the merry-go-round.

For a moment it seems that they will never get off the merry-go-round because it will never stop. I feel like one who looks down on the avenue from the 50th story of a building. But at length they do get off; even the music of the hand-organ has ceased for a moment. My father has acquired ten rings, my mother only two, although it was my mother who really wanted them.

They walk on along the boardwalk as the afternoon descends by imperceptible degrees into the incredible violet of dusk. Everything fades into a relaxed glow, even the ceaseless murmuring from the beach, and the revolutions of the merry-go-round. They look for a place to have dinner. My father suggests the best one on the boardwalk and my mother demurs, in accordance with her principles.

However they do go to the best place, asking for a table near the window, so that they can look out on the boardwalk and the mobile ocean. My father feels omnipotent as he places a quarter in the waiter's hand as he asks for a table. The place is crowded and here too there is music, this time from a kind of string trio. My father orders dinner with a fine confidence.

As the dinner is eaten, my father tells of his plans for the future, and my mother shows with expressive face how interested she is, and how impressed. My father becomes exultant. He is lifted up by the waltz that is being played, and his own future begins to intoxicate him. My father tells my mother that he is going to expand his business, for there is a great deal of money to be made. He wants to settle down. After all, he is twenty-nine, he has lived by himself since he was thirteen, he is making more and more money, and he is envious of his married friends when he visits them in the cozy security of their homes, surrounded, it seems, by the calm domestic pleasures, and by delightful children, and then, as the waltz reaches the moment when all the dancers swing madly, then, then with awful daring, then he asks my mother to marry him, although awkwardly enough and puzzled, even in his excitement, at how he had arrived at the proposal, and she, to make the whole business worse, begins to cry, and my father looks nervously about, not knowing at all what to do now, and my mother says: "It's all I've wanted from the moment I saw you," sobbing, and he finds all of this very difficult, scarcely to his taste, scarcely as he had thought it would be, on his long walks over Brooklyn Bridge in the revery of a fine cigar, and it was then that I stood up in the theatre and shouted: "Don't do it. It's not too late to change your minds, both of you. Nothing good will come of it, only remorse, hatred, scandal, and two children whose characters are monstrous." The whole audience turned to look at me, annoyed, the usher came hurrying down the aisle flashing his searchlight, and the old lady next to me tugged me down into my seat, saying: "Be quiet. You'll be put out, and you paid thirty-five cents to come in." And so I shut my eyes because I could not bear to see what was happening. I sat there quietly.

V

But after awhile I begin to take brief glimpses, and at length I watch again with thirsty interest, like a child who wants to maintain his sulk although offered the bribe of candy. My parents are now having their picture taken in a photographer's booth along the boardwalk. The place is shadowed in the mauve light which is apparently necessary. The camera is set to the side on its tripod and looks like a Martian man. The photographer is instructing my parents in how to pose. My father has his arm over my mother's shoulder, and both of them smile emphatically. The photographer brings my mother a bouquet of flowers to hold in her hand but she holds it at the wrong angle. Then the photographer covers himself with the black cloth which drapes the camera and all that one sees of him is one protruding arm and his hand which clutches the rubber ball which he will squeeze when the picture is finally taken. But he is not satisfied with their appearance. He feels with certainty that somehow there is something wrong in their pose. Again and again he issues from his hidden place with

41

new directions. Each suggestion merely makes matters worse. My father is becoming impatient. They try a seated pose. The photographer explains that he has pride, he is not interested in all of this for the money, he wants to make beautiful pictures. My father says: "Hurry up, will you? We haven't got all night." But the photographer only scurries about apologetically, and issues new directions. The photographer charms me. I approve of him with all my heart, for I know just how he feels, and as he criticizes each revised pose according to some unknown idea of rightness, I become quite hopeful. But then my father says angrily: "Come on, you've had enough time, we're not going to wait any longer." And the photographer, sighing unhappily, goes back under his black covering, holds out his hand, says: "One, two, three, Now!", and the picture is taken, with my father's smile turned to a grimace and my mother's bright and false. It takes a few minutes for the picture to be developed and as my parents sit in the curious light they become quite depressed.

VI

They have passed a fortune-teller's booth, and my mother wishes to go in, but my father does not. They begin to argue about it. My mother becomes stubborn, my father once more impatient, and then they begin to quarrel, and what my father would like to do is walk off and leave my mother there, but he knows that that would never do. My mother refuses to budge. She is near to tears, but she feels an uncontrollable desire to hear what the palm-reader will say. My father consents angrily, and they both go into a booth which is in a way like the photographer's, since it is draped in black cloth and its light is shadowed. The place is too warm, and my father keeps saying this is all nonsense, pointing to the crystal ball on

42

the table. The fortuneteller, a fat, short woman, garbed in what is supposed to be Oriental robes, comes into the room from the back and greets them, speaking with an accent. But suddenly my father feels that the whole thing is intolerable; he tugs at my mother's arm, but my mother refuses to budge. And then, in terrible anger, my father lets go of my mother's arm and strides out, leaving my mother stunned. She moves to go after my father, but the fortune-teller holds her arm tightly and begs her not to do so, and I in my seat am shocked more than can ever be said, for I feel as if I were walking a tight-rope a hundred feet over a circus-audience and suddenly the rope is showing signs of breaking, and I get up from my seat and begin to shout once more the first words I can think of to communicate my terrible fear and once more the usher comes hurrying down the aisle flashing his searchlight, and the old lady pleads with me, and the shocked audience has turned to stare at me, and I keep shouting: "What are they doing? Don't they know what they are doing? Why doesn't my mother go after my father? If she does not do that, what will she do? Doesn't my father know what he is doing?"—But the usher has seized my arm and is dragging me away, and as he does so, he says: "What are *you* doing? Don't you know that you can't do whatever you want to do? Why should a young man like you, with your whole life before you, get hysterical like this? Why don't you *think* of what you're doing? You can't act like this even if other people aren't around! You will be sorry if you do not do what you should do, you can't carry on like this, it is not right, you will find that out soon enough, everything you do matters too much," and he said that dragging me through the lobby of the theatre into the cold light, and I woke up into the bleak winter morning of my 21st birthday, the windowsill shining with its lip of snow, and the morning already begun.

43

Screeno

For three hours, Cornelius Schmidt attempted to raise himself from the will-lessness and despondency which had overcome him. He tried to read the *New York Times,* which today contained the long obituary of a great man, the only kind of story that could awaken any interest in him. He played records on his portable victrola, first a string quartet by Haydn, and then, tiring of this with the third record, playing certain singing records of a celebrated movie actress. But to no avail: the music was lifeless as his own spirit. He then resorted, as often before in such a mood, to the icebox, making for himself a fat sandwich out of materials which would have otherwise not appealed to him. Having eaten the sandwich, he seated himself by the window and watched the quiet October evening rain soundlessly falling through the bright arc of the street light downstairs, four floors below, and pocking and wrinkling the glittering puddles. Automobiles passed with the frying sound which tires make on wet streets. Cornelius took down a volume of poetry of which he was very fond and tried to read it. A poem of his own slipped from the book. He read the first few verses and shuddered, thoroughly disheartened. Drenched by such a tasteless, colorless mood, there was only one refuge, one sanctuary: the movies.

He left a note for his mother on the kitchen table, donned his trench coat, and departed. Anticipation of the movie to be seen already began to rise in his breast. People in the huddled posture which rain enforces passed him as he walked to the business avenue where stores shone wetly

44

and brightly in the rainy night. Two boys were standing outside a candy store and trying to get chewing gum from the box beside the newsstand. Cornelius, in his rising spirits, was tempted to stop and afford them the benefit of his childhood talent for such efforts, his ability to make the machine give freely by a certain trick. But he knew that the boys would merely be shy, or afraid of him, and perhaps even antagonistic. At the age of twenty-five, he said to himself, I am neither here nor there, and can no longer expect to return with ease to the world of the young, that cruel zoo inhabited by a special kind of animal.

He came to the arcade of the movie house, reading the titles printed in electric bulbs framed by other lights which raced backward and forward along the arcade.

> JOHN BOLES AND EVELYN LAYE
> IN ONE HEAVENLY NIGHT ALSO
> SPENCER TRACY IN FREEDOM
> SCREENO TONIGHT $475 CASH

The presence of the new lottery annoyed him, for it meant an interruption in the flow of movies while the stage was lit and everyone looked about dazedly. At such times, Cornelius slouched far down in his seat, ashamed for some reason to be at the theatre alone, as if it were a confession of a lack of friends and engaging activities. But Spencer Tracy was an actor who had often pleased him by an absolute unself-consciousness, and Cornelius wished also to permit himself to be moved by the operetta music. Decided, he walked toward the box office, as a stream of people came out of the darkness of the theatre, looking like sleepwalkers.

At the door the uniformed ticket taker gave him a card on which was printed a kind of checkerboard, having in each box a number. It was obviously the old game of Lotto, the object being to get five numbers which were successive either horizontally or vertically or in a diagonal. In the center, amid numbered boxes, was a box entitled GRATIS; the management gave this box to the audience.

Cornelius completed his examination of this card while walking on the eerie soundless plush carpet of the stupendous lobby, from whose lofty top great chandeliers hung. In a moment, he was in the midst of the ghostly evening of the theatre; two thousand entranced persons stared toward the white and black screen, ignorant of all else. A harried usher led him to an aisle in the middle of the theatre and hastily departed. Once free of the usher, Cornelius walked further down, blind in the soft darkness after the recent blaze of chandeliers, and after some trouble found himself the kind of seat he wanted, one in the middle of the aisle, where he would not be disturbed by those who wished to depart.

Located in his seat, and comfortable at last, Cornelius directed his gaze toward the screen. The newsreel was on, and cavalrymen were leaping high barriers, flying upward from the saddle at the apex of the jump and then settling back again, all of this performed with no little grace. The unseen voice, the commentator who always made Cornelius remember the Oracle at Delphi, was saying: "Uncle Sam does not intend to be unprepared." The scene shifted suddenly, to the accompaniment of sad and heavy music. Flood pictures were shown; a family departed from its almost submerged frame house in a rowboat, the young son of the family clutching his dog in his arms. The face of the dog and of the boy was shown in a close-up. The bleak and baffled look of the dog charmed the audience. Everything moved slowly in the slowly moving water. The commentator stated his sentiments in a histri-

46

onic baritone: "Nature shows its might on the Ohio. Thousands are left homeless by the cruel and raging waters." And then with a montage of archetypal newsreel scenes (West Point; a batter swinging; Roosevelt at the microphone; an actress descending from a train) and a martial music which came to a ringing close, the newsreel was ended. The theatre lightened and a well-dressed young man came upon the stage before the screen, carrying a microphone with him. The uniformed ushers followed him. In the corner stood a round red poster to which golden discs were attached. When you turned the disc over, the amount of money you had won was revealed by the dollar sign upon the disc.

"Good evening, ladies and gentlemen," said the young man, speaking into the microphone with a knowing and efficient tone. "The management is again glad to offer prizes for the winners in SCREENO. Again we are offering $425 for anyone who gets SCREENO with the first seven numbers called. If no one is so fortunate, then we will add $25 to the amount and next week the sum will be $450. Besides this, $50 in prizes will be distributed tonight to the first ten people who get SCREENO. Now as soon as you have five consecutive numbers, either horizontally or vertically or in a diagonal, please call out loudly and clearly and come down to the stage. Then you will place your disc on the board and you will win some part of fifty dollars. Remember now! five numbers in a row! horizontal, vertical, diagonal. Good luck to all of you! And remember that everyone can't win."

True enough, said Cornelius to himself.

The theatre fell into a semi-darkness, not the movie darkness, but one in which discreet lights shone on both sides of the theatre and both sides of the stage. A white and pink clockface flashed on the screen. It was, in fact, like a roulette wheel, and had numbers running from 1 to

100. In the center was a pointer, which suddenly began to whirl furiously about the clockface, and then slowed down, and then stopped.

"Ninety-nine!" said the businesslike yet airy young man in an authoritative voice. An usher wrote down the number upon a blackboard to the right of the screen. The pointer spun again, at a tremendous pace, so that it was almost a moving blur for a moment, and then clarified into its arrow-like straightness. The actual wheel was, of course, in the projection room.

"Fifty-four!" said the young master of ceremonies, simulating a dramatic tone.

"SCREENO!" cried a voice from the balcony in a mocking voice, while everyone laughed, for obviously no one could have SCREENO as yet.

"I am sorry, ladies and gentlemen," said the young man in an affable voice, "but we will have to ask you not to be humorous about this. After all, money is involved, and there has been much confusion in the past because various people insisted upon trying to be funny."

"All right, Senator," cried the same balcony voice, and the audience laughed again. Meanwhile Cornelius had become very interested. He had both of the first two numbers and had marked them by pushing his finger through the soft cardboard of each box. It would be curious indeed, he said to himself, if I won. Probably no one here could make better use of the $425. But I have never been lucky and I am certainly not a prize-winner.

The pointer was revolving again. 'Thirty-nine!" announced the young man. The audience was not yet warmed up, because too few numbers had been called for anyone to be on the verge of winning. Cornelius, however, also had this third number and was pleased no little by the course of events.

"Forty-nine!" announced the young man.

"Raspberries!" cried the same voice from the balcony.

"Please!" said the young man in a tone of unctuous and good-natured irony, "I must ask you to restrain yourself, my dear friend in the balcony. Otherwise we will be forced to suppose that you are intoxicated, and since there are more suitable places than this for those in that state, we will have to ask you to leave. Your money will be refunded."

"I won't go. I've been kicked out of better places than this," said the balcony voice. The young master of ceremonies signalled to one of the ushers, indicating the necessity of action. Cornelius had paid little attention to the disturbance, for the number forty-nine was on his card also. He needed only one more number in order to win, and was enormously excited. He felt that something was about to go wrong; good fortune was always too precarious, too contingent, too arbitrary an event to be, in truth, good fortune. *Non forat ullum illaesa felicitas,* (unbroken prosperity is unable to bear any evil—if I have translated Seneca correctly). The disturbance from the balcony impressed him immediately as a possible source of reversal and he turned a resentful face toward the balcony, faced forward again, and waited for the pointer to turn again. It did.

"Eight!" cried the young master of ceremonies. A hasty glance convinced Cornelius that he did not have the number. Two more chances to win the big prize, and buy fifty volumes in the Loeb Classical Library. The pointer turned weakly this time.

"Fourteen!" cried the young man into the microphone which made his voice even more official than otherwise. Cornelius did not have the number. He assured himself that the game was a fraud, that the management was obviously not going to permit anyone to win so much money and that the whole business would obviously be controlled in the projection room or by arranging the

49

numbers on the cards. There was only one more chance, a drop in the ocean. He slouched back in his seat, chiding himself for his great excitement.

Meanwhile the pointer was turning quickly, and then weakly.

"Twenty-five!" the master of ceremonies called out.

"Twenty-five! Twenty-five!" said Cornelius to himself, and then, finding the number on his card as the fifth consecutive horizontal number, he rose in his seat and shouted:

"SCREENO!" in a too loud voice which broke, and began to issue from his aisle, tripping over the feet of the people seated near him, some of whom were solicitous of his walk, and eager to provide good advice as he passed. The attractiveness of the winner shone in him.

"Twenty-five! Twenty-five!" said Cornelius to himself. "My age! My gold mine!" He felt the eyes of the whole immense audience upon him as he walked to the stage and the self-consciousness which had always tortured him made him walk with too careful steps.

An usher took his card, and checked it with the numbers on the blackboard. The young man came over to oversee the usher. It seemed as if something was wrong, someone had miscalculated, to look at the young man. The checking was done several times. Very bureaucratic, said Cornelius to himself. Recovering, as the checkup proved that Cornelius had indeed won, he shook Cornelius's hand and the whole theatre lighted up.

"Lucky fellow," cried the balcony voice, amusing the audience again, by the envious tone in his voice.

"Congratulations," the young man said, "the sum of $425 is yours." He led Cornelius before the microphone. "Now before I pay you, will you tell us your name and address.

"Cornelius Schmidt," whispered Cornelius (the whis-

per, but not the words resounded in the microphone).
"845 West 163rd Street."

The young man repeated this information into the microphone as if it were a matter of great importance.

"Cornelius Vanderbilt," shouted the balcony wit, "Park Avenue."

"And what do you do?" the young man asked both Cornelius and the microphone, as if no one could do anything which would not come under his authority.

"Oh," said Cornelius, "I do many things," into the microphone.

The audience laughed, and Cornelius, pleased, grinned in spite of himself. But he was uneasy. He did not wish to tell the truth, that he was a writer, for he was an unknown writer, and besides the profession always appeared to him as seeming peculiar and anomalous to others. On the other hand, he did not want to say he was unemployed, his usual subterfuge, because that also seemed a shameful admission. And then he was ashamed of himself, angered at himself for not wishing to tell the truth, for being ashamed of a noble calling, so that he forced himself to the other extreme, and specified his kind of writing and told the functionary that he was a poet. He knew this would be equivalent to sissy or bohemian for some of the audience.

"Mr. Schmidt is a poet," announced the young man unctuously, patronizingly, and then, desiring to be humorous himself, he spoke cutely into the microphone:

> He's a poet,
> His feet show it,
> They're Longfellow's!

The audience roared as the young man drew out the last word with a triumphant tone, and Cornelius blushed and wished he were elsewhere, and became extremely angered at the young man, who had previously merely annoyed him. As a matter of fact, Cornelius's feet were by no means small, and, becoming still more self-conscious, he tried to withdraw his shoes somehow from public view.

"I am sure we would like to hear one of the poems of so fortunate a young man," said the official young man. He was trying to delay matters until one of the ushers could bring enough money from the box office to pay Cornelius. "Please," he said, "recite some verses for us."

"Oh, no!" said Cornelius firmly, backing away. The young man gestured to the intrigued audience which then began to applaud in unison to express its desire to hear Cornelius recite his verses.

Angered again, and in his anger going again to the other extreme, Cornelius decided to recite for them. All of his happiness in winning had disappeared, and a mood of stubborn resentment had come upon him.

"Very well," he said harshly into the microphone. "I will recite some appropriate verses for you." Changing his tone to one of serious and dramatic import, and permitting a certain implication of tiredness, illness, and despair to creep into his voice, he began:

> Think now
> History has many cunning passages, contrived corridors
> And issues, deceives with whispering ambitions,
> Guides us by vanities. Think now
> She gives when our attention is distracted
> And what she gives, gives with such supple confusions
> That the giving famishes the craving. Gives too late
> What's not believed in, or if still believed,
> In memory only, reconsidered passion. Gives too soon
> Into weak hands, what's thought can be dispensed with
> Till the refusal propagates a fear.

He ended appalled at himself, as if he had made a shocking confession. But he saw that his effort was a failure for his tone had been false, too serious. The audience had been silenced and puzzled by the verses, but the young man, curiously enough, had been impressed.

"Are those your own verses?" he asked.

"No. I wish they were," said Cornelius. The audience wakened at this and laughed.

"Those verses were written by the best of modern poets," said Cornelius, "a man named T. S. Eliot, whom all of you ought to read." Even in saying this, Cornelius knew that this advertisement was a foolish thing.

The usher arrived with the money just as the persistent balcony voice called out, "Let's go on with the show," and the audience began to clap again, wishing to have its chance at the other prizes.

But then, as the money was delivered to the young assistant manager, and he began officiously to count it out, shuffle it, and arrange it, before paying Cornelius, a hoarse and disused voice cried from the balcony:

"SCREENO! SCREENO!"

A silence fell upon all, and all turned backward to look for the author of the impassioned outcry.

"SCREENO!" came the voice again, this time nearer, as the new winner approached the stairs from the balcony to the orchestra. The young assistant manager and the ushers looked at each other in dismay. Something had obviously gone wrong, for usually no one won the jackpot; two winners was inconceivable and would lead to bankruptcy. Someone was going to lose his job because of this.

In a moment, the new winner was on the stage. He was a small and slight old man, carrying a violin case and wearing glasses. In his unpressed black suit, he looked very much like a waiter in a cheap restaurant. He was completely out of breath, completely beside himself. An usher took his card from his quavering hand and began to check it with the numbers on the blackboard. The young assistant manager came over to superintend the checking, obviously hoping for some mistake. Meanwhile, Cornelius stood by suddenly ignored, having nothing to do. He had not yet been given his money, but was blissful with ideas of its expenditure.

"If the manager loses all this money," said one usher to another, "it will be the biggest collapse since the Fall of the Hapsburgs.

"My name is Casper Weingarten," said the old man, unasked, intruding himself upon the huddle of the assistant manager and the ushers. He was very nervous, very excited. "I am a musician," he said, but no one paid any attention to him, except Cornelius.

And then the young assistant manager came over to the old man and, holding the card up, showed him that he had not won, that he had mistaken a 7 for a 1 because the print had been on the left-hand side. "Perhaps you'll win one of the other prizes," he said, courteously, "since you already have four numbers in a row."

"You mean I don't win?" said the old man. "Why not?" he said, having understood nothing of the explanation. His mistake was explained again, while he stared at his card.

"No!" he said loudly. "This is a 1, not a 7. I win. Give me my money." His voice was weak and now that he raised it, it was curiously pathetic, and like the voice of an angry child. And to make matters worse, he began to cough.

"My dear man," said the assistant manager, resuming his official tone, "I am sorry but you are mistaken. You have not won. You have mistaken a 7 for a 1 because the print was faint. After this, all of the cards will be clearly printed, so that such mistakes cannot occur.

Cornelius came over to look into the matter for himself. He took the card in his hand and looked at the number in question. The old man looked at him, and then turned to the assistant manager, saying:

"Give me my money! I have won!"

"You are being very unreasonable," said the assistant manager, beginning to look harassed. The audience now began to clap to indicate its desire for proceeding with the rest of the game. The assistant manager explained what had happened to the audience with great care and tact.

"Give me my money!" shouted the old man, as the young man was speaking to the audience.

"Please return to your seat," he said to the old man, "so that the game can go on."

Meanwhile Cornelius had looked carefully at the number in question and decided that the assistant manager had no ground for deciding that the 1 was a 7. There was a blur beside the upright bar of 1 which might conceivably have been meant to be the horizontal bar which completed the 7, but the faintness of the blur was not sufficient to justify the assistant manager.

"Look here," said Cornelius tactfully to the assistant manager, "it seems to me that you can only assume that this is a 1. The blur is too faint to make it a seven.

"I know it is a 7," said the assistant manager angrily, and when he said that, Cornelius recognized immediately that he was so sure because the cards had been prepared in advance to obviate the possibility of two winners of the jackpot, or even one. Seeing this, Cornelius began to feel sick and angry, as he always did when confronted with fraud or cheating.

"All my life I've been cheated," said the old man, wringing his hands. "Give me my money." An usher took his arm, as if to lead him from the stage, but the assistant manager deterred him, unwilling as yet to resort to force.

"Look here," said Cornelius firmly, "either you pay him or I am going to speak to the audience about this." In reply, the assistant manager began to pay Cornelius, counting the money with clipped tones as he placed it in Cornelius's hand. The old man grabbed the assistant manager's arm when he finished, saying:

"Where is my money? Don't cheat me, I've had hard luck all my life."

"My good man," said the assistant manager, "Your hard luck is not my fault, nor this theatre's responsibility. Please do not cause a disturbance. Now if both of you will leave the stage, we can go on with the other prizes and with the show."

In answer, the old man sat down upon the stage, looking grotesque there, with his head turned up. "I will sit here until I am paid," he said tearfully.

The scene was becoming unbearable for Cornelius. The old man seemed to have decided that this money was as important as his life. As far as Cornelius was concerned, he had been cheated. This was too much for Cornelius.

"I am going to tell the audience about this," said Cornelius.

"No, you're not," said the assistant manager, but Cornelius reached the microphone before the assistant manager could get there.

"Listen!" said the assistant manager, in a wearied breathless panicky voice, "I'm going to lose my job for this. Have a heart."

This new object of sympathy made matters even more complex for Cornelius. But then he looked toward the old man seated on the floor. He had begun sobbing, and he had taken off his glasses, wet by his tears, and was drying them with a rumpled handkerchief.

This sight decided Cornelius. He grasped the microphone and addressed the audience.

"Ladies and gentlemen, the management refuses to pay this man the sum which he has won, claiming that his card was badly printed. This is only a pretext. I have examined the card and there is no justification for the management's claim. The management is trying to welch on its obligation."

The assistant manager stepped forward immediately to reply. Cornelius's speech had obviously had a genuine effect.

"Ladies and gentlemen, this young man may be adept at poetry, but he cannot see what is directly in front of him. He is attempting to take advantage of the management's generosity. Not satisfied with having won the sum of $425, he is trying to get a similar sum for someone he has just encountered. Meanwhile it is becoming late, and if this stage is not cleared immediately, it will be necessary to postpone the plans for the remaining prizes. The operator in the projection room is a union man and cannot be persuaded to remain a moment overtime; and since we cannot postpone pictures, we will have to postpone the remaining prizes unless these gentlemen leave immediately."

"You're a fine manager," cried the balcony wit.

But the audience was won over, for no one wished to lose his chance at the remaining $50. There was a murmuring of voices and someone cried out:

"Go home and give us a chance."

"Ladies and gentlemen," said the old man in a broken voice. He had arisen upon seeing the effect of the manager's speech. "These people are trying to cheat me. I have won. I am a musician. I would not do anything dishonest even if I am only a musician in a restaurant," sobbing, "this has always happened to me when something good should have happened. There was a quarrel at my daughter's wedding, the happiest day of my life. Now I have to live with my daughter-in-law," and still sobbing, "I could have my teeth fixed with the money. They have been bad for years. Don't let them cheat me."

A counter-reaction spread, although the vulgar reference to teeth had been unfortunate. Cornelius was prepared to commit any act in order to bring a halt to the old man's sobbing: scenes, rows, disturbances in public places had always had a direct solar plexus effect upon him.

"This is a bottomless pit," said one usher to another.

"Ladies and gentlemen," said the assistant manager, "although we are convinced that we are right, we are ready to put this whole matter into the hands of a committee of three objective members of the audience."

"Oh," said Cornelius to himself, "they are going to start the whole objective and subjective business again."

There was a pause while three members of the audience were solicited to act as judges. The assistant manager, still attempting to maintain his benevolence, offered free theatre tickets for the following week as reward for jury service. A dentist, a lawyer, and the owner of a haberdashery store came forward. The dentist, a sympathetic man, immediately offered to fix Weingarten's teeth cheap, for a nominal sum. The old man ignored the offer, offending the dentist.

"Give me my money," he said weakly, almost an echo of his former voice.

The committee was given the disputed card and went into a conference in a corner. But before they had been there long, an enterprising usher found another card on which the 1 had been printed with a blur next to it. The card was brought up to the stage and in a moment everything was settled once and for all.

The assistant manager announced the discovery. The lawyer announced the committee's decision. The audience applauded, satisfied that justice had been done. Casper

Weingarten sat down on the stage again. Cornelius looked helplessly about him, and the audience began to clap and hoot.

"Why don't you go home," said one.

"Call a cop," said another.

Cornelius stepped forth and said, painstakingly, "Can't you see that the fact that two cards have the same blur on them proves nothing. It may be a 1 in both cases. You are permitting yourselves to be deceived."

But the audience had decided once and for all. It was now intent upon going on with the game and then on with the show, and answered Cornelius by hoots and whistles. The ushers came forward.

And then, threatened by the ushers, Cornelius made the worst mistake.

"Be logical," he said angrily, "don't be hopelessly middle class about this. The management is trying to cheat an old man."

"This poet is a radical," said the assistant manager, seeing his opportunity to win a complete victory. "You heard what he just said: middle class. He is a radical."

"C.I.O.," called the balcony wit, with a rising inflection on the O, as one would say "I'll be seeing *you*." The audience giggled, enchanted by this, and the cry was taken up immediately.

"C.I.O. C.I.O. C.I.O.," came various voices throughout the house.

Cornelius recognized that nothing more could be done with the audience. He went over to the old musician, still seated upon the floor and drying his glasses again, for he was still weeping.

'Look, old man," said Cornelius, "there's nothing to be done about this. You'd better come with me."

"No," said Weingarten, categorically.

Cornelius meditated with himself for a moment and

then said: "Listen, I will give you half of the jackpot. Come on before you're arrested."

"Call a cop," cried the same voice that had previously made this suggestion.

"No," said Weingarten, "I don't want your money. I want mine. Give me my money," he said towards the assistant manager.

Cornelius considered matters with himself again and came to a decision. Easy come, easy go, he said to himself, and then he told the old musician that he could have the whole jackpot. The manager protested immediately, but Cornelius took the bills from his pocket and began to count them out and give them to the musician, who accepted them with a guilty look and trembling hands.

The audience saw what was happening and applauded vigorously, not because it was genuinely moved, but because it felt that it ought to applaud. Such applause is heard at public gatherings when an abstraction too vacuous is mentioned or tribute is paid to a man long dead. The assistant manager, trying to move in on Cornelius's credit, came over to shake hands with Cornelius. Cornelius, tempted to reject the proffered hand, accepted it because he wished to cause no further disturbance.

The old man had risen and come over to Cornelius.

"Thank you very much for your kindness," he said in the estranged voice of those who have been weeping or overexcited.

"Not at all," said Cornelius formally. Both descended from the stage together.

"We will have to forego the remaining prizes until next week," said the assistant manager, "but the fifty dollars will be added to next week's total, and there will be a hundred dollars in prizes besides the usual jackpot. In addition, two four-star pictures will be playing."

The theatre darkened as Cornelius and Weingarten walked to the exits, the film went on with all its soft floating figures and pleasing movement. How much actuality, after all, can an audience stand in the course of one evening?

"Are you going my way?" said Cornelius to Weingarten.

"No, I think I'll see the rest of the show. Thank you very much, much obliged," he said, still weighed by guilt.

The problem now, said Cornelius to himself as he walked through the soft carpeted lobby, is to keep this from my mother, who will consider me quixotic, as indeed I am. But how small a price for the sense of generosity and dignity which I now have, even though the act was forced upon me by my maudlin sympathy for the old man. Probably I have been foolish, and yet how reasonable I feel at present, and how joyous.

Saying this, in his joy, he issued into the chill and disorder of the street, the fresh air and different light striking him. The rain had ceased, but a thick fog had come upon the city. And as he walked home through this fog, in a pure enjoyment of his feeling, Cornelius recited to himself this poem by a fourteenth-century Scottish poet, halting sometimes in the middle of a line because he did not remember it too well, or halting in order to correct his imperfect accent:

Be merry, man! and tak not sair in mind
    The wavering of this wretched world of sorrow!
To God be humble and to thy friend be kind,
    And with thy neighbors gladly lend and borrow:
His chance to-nicht, it may be thine tomorrow;
    Be blithe in heart for ony adventure;
For oft with wise men, 't has been said aforrow,

Without gladness availis no treasure.

Mak thee gude cheer of it that God thee sends,
    For wand's wrack but welfare nocht avails.
No gude is thine, save only that thou spends;
    Remanent all thou brookis but with bales.
Seek to solace when sadness thee assails;
    In dolour long thy life may not endure,
Wherefore of comfort set up all thy sails;
Without gladness avails no treasure.

Follow on pity, flee trouble and debate,
    With famous folk aye hold thy company;
Be charitable and humble in thy estate,
    For wardly honour lastes but a cry;
For trouble in earth take no melancholy;
    Be rich in patience, if thou in goods be poor;
Who lives merry he lives michtily;
Without gladness avails no treasure.

So saying, joyous, with a sense of having done proud-
ly what he wanted to do, and with the fog hiding from
him most of the street and surrounding his head, he came
back to his house and the room where he would be once
more alone.

The Heights of Joy

Infatuation is not exactly the right word to describe the feelings of Hugo Bauer, the financier, when he first looked at Magda Gehrhardt, the great beauty of stage and films who was to become his wife. He saw her for the first time at an embassy reception in Paris; a great many people were present and he saw her from a distance, surrounded by a circle of admirers. To most of them she seemed—as she seemed to Hugo Bauer—a fabulous being, a divinity whom one hardly supposed to be a human being. Her images were everywhere: the perfection of her face appeared not only on the screen, in the hypnotized darkness of the motion picture cathedral, but one came upon it unexpectedly and yet constantly, on magazine covers, in the exaggerated vividness of advertisements, in sleek photographs of picture periodicals, or upon billboard posters, gigantically enlarged and yet undiminished in the beauty and serenity of her countenance.

The astonished admiration Hugo Bauer felt was unlike the experience of love, any phase of the experience of love: it was not like falling in love at first sight, for Hugo Bauer's sense of dazzled astonishment not only excluded all thought of desire and of making love, but it was inconceivable, then, for Hugo Bauer to think of conversing with so beautiful and so self-possessed a being.

Hugo Bauer's rapt look, his sudden uncharacteristic loss of self-composure—his complete disregard of those who surrounded him because he was a person of great power, feared by governments and international cartels-was so enchanted a look that it was noticed by a young man standing near him who knew Magda Gehrhardt: he was sufficiently struck by the extent to which Hugo Bauer was impressed to tell the actress how dazzled Hugo Bauer had been. The young man told Magda Gehrhardt that she had made a conquest of a special kind, and he explained to her how important Hugo Bauer was. Since she was so used to being regarded as an idol, one more conquest, one more man in a state of adoration, would have meant very little to her by itself. What did interest and please her, somewhat to her own perplexity, was to learn that she had won the admiration of a man who was far more important and powerful than the presidents, prime ministers and kings of most nations.

The pleasure she felt continued to surprise her after her informant had departed. She found herself in a state of tantalized interest, an exciting and demanding curiosity about what kind of man Hugo Bauer was. He had departed from the embassy reception soon after arriving, making no effort to speak to her. He acted very unlike all the other men of wealth and power when they encountered and were wonderstruck by her radiance. The following morning, when she found herself still interested, pleased, and curious, she wrote to Hugo Bauer, inviting him to call upon her, expecting that as always—however slight or passing her interest in a man—he would respond to her note very quickly, particularly since she herself had taken the initiative and suggested an immediate answer by sending a special messenger.

Several hours passed as Magda awaited an answer; and she felt full of anticipation and wholly delighted during the time her note remained unanswered; and when at last, an answer arrived, it turned her curiosity into a kind of insatiable intoxication. The answer was typed and had been signed by Hugo Bauer's secretary: it said with the utmost formality that Mr. Bauer had left Paris that day, wished to thank her for the kindness of her note, and would look forward to a meeting in the future whenever he was again in the same city as Miss Gehrhardt.

Magda's amazement united with the curiosity she had felt all day and became genuine fascination of a peculiar kind. She had been the object of pursuit for years and her suitors had been ardent, craven, passionate, patient, servile, ingenious, poetic, arrogant, cruel and desperate. Some had promised her more than anyone possessed, inexhaustible opulence or endless adoration; others had threatened her, abused her, written or spoken erotic words that verged on the obscene, threatened suicide or murder and suicide; and some had combined these actions at various passages of courtship. But never before had a man responded to an open expression of interest, in which she herself was bold and made the first move, by answering as Hugo Bauer had answered her, sending her a typed note written by another and making his departure to a distant city, and thus, by going far away, suggesting an indifference or preoccupation—whichever it was—to her as a desirable being. However she looked at the note, she could not deny the likelihood that Hugo Bauer had been neither interested nor flattered by her invitation.

II

Magda's note pleased Hugo Bauer very much, but did not seem flattering to him. His departure had been planned the week before: yet it might have been postponed with ease. When Hugo had received the film star's note, he had looked at it for a long time and had been bemused to think of what hopes it would have excited in him in his first youth, before he had renounced all possibility of romantic love: now that he was forty-seven years of age, it was hardly possible for him to believe that personal attractiveness—which he had not possessed even in his first youth—rather than the exaggerated fame of his wealth and power had made so beautiful a woman—and one who was twenty or thirty years younger—write to him and ask him to call upon her.

Yet, as he looked from the train window at the passing countryside and moved farther and farther from Paris, he found himself unable to forget Magda Gehrhardt, the radiance and the perfection of her image, at the embassy reception the day before. Whatever he saw, looking idly from the train window, suggested that image in one or another way: once as the train stopped at a small station in the foothills of the Alps, he was sure, for one astounded moment, that he was looking at Magda, walking out of the station, followed by a servant, and moving toward a cab: then, as the young woman stooped to enter the cab, he was just as sure that it was not Magda, just as, a second before, he had been sure that he was looking at her. Her face remained turned away from him throughout: the slight alteration of her body as she stooped to enter the cab was enough to make him aware of how wrong he had been, and thus of the extent to which he had fallen in love, despite himself.

The remarkable tenderness that swelled in him then was an emotion he had not known since the age of twenty-four, at a time when he was still quite poor. He had been very much in love then, with a young, waitress: it was in Vienna, at a time when it was virtually customary to be in love. One night, he waited for the pretty waitress to meet him at the table of an inexpensive restaurant, he had been so nervous and impatient, he had looked so eagerly and with so much excitement, expectation and the beginning of relief toward each opening of the door of the entrance, and then had experienced so much obvious disappointment when the newcomer failed to be the one he awaited with so much excited impatience—that one waiter, who had noticed the intensity of his vigil, said to another: "If the lady does not appear quite soon, I will have to give him my own girl: anything less would be inhuman cruelty; and the only other possible form of kindness would be to put a bullet through his head, as with a horse who has broken his leg. Nothing less would end his suffering."

The waiter unknowingly had spoken too clearly and loudly. Hugo had overheard him, had looked at his watch and seen how late the girl was—she was very late indeed—and then had left the restaurant abruptly, suddenly overcome by a sense of how ridiculous he appeared, how much of an infatuated adolescent he was. He had never communicated with the girl again and her failure to try to communicate with him had been the final evidence of his foolishness. Thenceforward he did not permit himself to entertain any thought of romantic love, telling himself again and again that it was an emotion that devoured all of one's waking life and might very well destroy one: moreover, it was an attitude that no human being, however attractive, justified: no woman, however desirable or beautiful, remained for very long a desirable and beautiful being. Romantic love was a summer thunderstorm and passed quickly. If one were careful, one would not be struck by lightning. And every human being, Hugo had long since decided, is too weak, too frail, too mortal, to make romantic love anything but lunacy. And besides there are too many others, so that it is indeed extremely foolish and harmful to attach a unique importance to any particular one among the many.

Soon after he came to this conclusion, Hugo Bauer began to grow very rich. He was sometimes asked, as his wealth increased, if he ever intended to marry. The passing affairs with various attractive women seemed to his friends to resemble vacations, excursions and rest-cures. And he seemed to those who knew him, a man who really wanted to exist in a state of marriage and domestic comfort. Hugo's answer, whenever he was questioned through the years, had been ironic, deliberately meant to conceal the wound of his first youth that he still felt from time to time, when he was exhausted or just waking from a dream. He had said again and again to those who questioned him: "A rolling stone gathers no remorse." He knew that no one was deceived, since he was not a being given to remorse, but this concealed his intimate feelings.

Now for the first time since his humiliation, Hugo felt again as he had felt so long ago, awaiting the tardy young woman. And now he had no reason to fear that love would become an obsession that took too much time so that all other aims were neglected or left unfulfilled. On the other hand, he had more reason now to fear the rejection of his devotion and love.

Nevertheless, for the time being he set aside the conviction that whatever reason Magda Gehrhardt had had to write him, it was not a reason that would be pleasing. It was and it had been foolish to permit one rejection by one young woman to cause so much withdrawal, for so many years. Hence, when the train arrived at its destination, at midnight, Hugo Bauer altered his plans and took the very next train back to Paris, determined to see the actress as soon as he had arrived in the French capital.

III

In Paris, Hugo Bauer consulted his invaluable adviser and secretary, Vincent De Vries, telling him with much embarrassment, about his feelings for Magda, and asking him—an extraordinary act indeed—to tell him candidly whether or not he was being very foolish.

He was told that on the contrary there must have been a genuine interest on the actress' part: otherwise she would certainly not have written to him as she had, for she was surely not at a loss for admirers of every stripe and disposition, status and age.

This suggested to Hugo a course which he immediately set in motion: he would give a dinner party for Magda Gehrhardt, inviting a good many other guests, so that their first real meeting would not be too intense and too nervous, the state of being in which, increasingly, since meeting Magda, Hugo found himself, and one which was at once the cause of suffering and helplessness: he felt helpless and powerless to free himself of his own present emotions. It had been many years since he had felt powerless in any matter: the emotion was almost a novel one.

The dinner was arranged. Magda answered immediately, writing to Hugo Bauer that she would be delighted to come to the dinner party and expressing some surprise: she had not expected to hear from him again so soon, although she had desired to meet him very much.

IV

The dinner party had been planned with the utmost care: yet at first it threatened to be a fiasco. For Hugo Bauer behaved with the same shyness which had afflicted him when he was sixteen years of age. He made an effort to ignore the presence of the actress; and his shyness shamed him. He conversed with others in an absent-minded way, and although he glanced again and again at the great beauty (thinking that his glances were unperceived by her: she was amused, charmed, flattered, and touched when she perceived them) it was necessary for Magda Gehrhardt to take the initiative once again and engage Hugo Bauer in conversation. Bauer was pleased but paralyzed by the attentions of the actress: he became more shy than ever: he was quite aware that he was behaving very foolishly, but he did not realize that his behavior pleased and flattered Magda Gehrhardt very much. She had been surrounded and courted by clever, suave, handsome and poised men since the beginning of her career. Each of them had always turned out to be far more interested in himself than in her; however much they concealed this fact, it revealed itself in the pleasure each of them took in being seen in public with Magda, a pleasure greater, clearly, than in being with her in privacy and solitude.

She too was chiefly interested in herself—with an incomparable intensity, as she knew—and what she wanted—was a man who would be more interested in her than in himself and a man more interested in being alone with her than in being seen by others in her company and yet, at the same time, a man who would be important in his own right and in the eyes of the world. Hugo Bauer's stout and stocky appearance made him seem to himself an unattractive man since he supposed that women looked at men as men looked at women. But it was precisely this sense of himself which made Hugo Bauer very attractive to Magda Gehrhardt: his diffidence was virtually the physical equivalent of his great wealth and power. He had, moreover, a burly and bear-like dignity; his very shyness and nervousness made him all the more attractive and it was, she recognized, rooted in his admiration of her and his humility about being desirable himself. She soon felt certain that Hugo was the man she wanted to marry.

Once he was certain that the actress had encouraged him and was genuinely interested in him, Hugo Bauer courted her with a magnificent lavishness that his wealth made possible, which delighted him more than any other phase of courtship. His astonishment that Magda thought him a very interesting human being and one whom she would think of as a suitor vanished when he discussed his doubts with Vincent De Vries and was told that his wealth was certainly unimportant except as a symbol, since the actress herself earned a stupendous salary and had already set enough aside of her earnings to keep her in comfort the rest of her life. Vincent added, with much tact, that women, for the most parts, were not interested in good looks as men were: in fact, they were repelled by truly handsome young men almost as much as most men were fascinated by truly beautiful women. For women wanted something more important than physical attractiveness or physical beauty: they wanted a man who possessed power, or fame, or status. This gave a woman a sense of superiority and of security, a security which the quality of being handsome, far from achieving, tended to undermine or take away: a very handsome man was likely to be a peacock, too attractive to other women to be trusted all the time, and too satisfied with his own appearance to be ambitious and successful in his ambition.

Hugo Bauer was not entirely convinced by these remarks. He had always made a point of being very critical of any statement, or interpretation of matters, which pleased him. It was this kind of thinking and calculating which had helped to make him successful as a financier. It was only after doubt and hesitation that he recognized how wrong he was and in what way: he had regarded the pursuit of the actress just as he had thought of the pursuit of wealth and power; and as a financier he dealt with human beings who for the most part wanted precisely what he wanted: the few women with whom he had had financial dealings had behaved not as women, but as human beings who wanted money. He himself had never wanted fame—indeed he had feared it, with reason—yet fame had overtaken him as he became very rich. Now, after deceiving himself a good deal about her feelings, he saw that Magda Gehrhardt had from the beginning of her career sought fame, the fame of personal magnetism, and she was now looking for the same dazzling and intoxicating experience of fame, which she had already known from strangers and from the public, in her own private life. It was a sensation as enchanting as laughter and beyond the power of money; whether it was possible in the intimacy of love or marriage was, at best, questionable. But clearly this was what the actress wanted, the ovation of applause, the triumphal march of a Caesar or a conqueror, not in public, but in her own daily and private life. She had enjoyed this delight in her own radiance so much that she wanted it at all times and she thought she would get it from someone who, like Hugo Bauer, possessed great wealth and was possessed by adoration of her and diffidence about himself.

Magda Gehrhardt's pleasure in Hugo Bauer's extreme admiration soon became a consistent source of excitement to the young actress. Recognizing that it was self-doubt which made him hesitant, she was very kind and very patient. She drew him out in conversation; she made him tell her of his early career, and of his early experiences with young women, responding to what he told her so that what had seemed humiliating to him became comic, pathetic, and charming for the first time, since it was in this light that Magda viewed what had occurred to him. After Magda had waited for more than two months for Hugo to declare what had become quite obvious, she said to him sweetly, directly, modestly and candidly: "Do you know, I am in love with you?!" Hugo Bauer was tongue-tied and stupefied. His incredulity was as immense as his joy.

It was necessary to wait a while before the marriage of

the star and the financier could occur. During the delay, Hugo Bauer insisted on the utmost propriety; it was the first time since meeting Magda that he had ever enforced his own sense of what ought to be done instead of yielding immediately to her wishes. He refused to anticipate the consummation of the marriage, a delicacy which he did not explain and which consequently seemed to Magda, at first, ridiculous, and then suggested for a moment that her lover might suffer from some difficulty in making love. She had been told this was all too common, for a brief period, in men of his age. But when Magda understood that for Hugo, it was a question of observing the utmost propriety, since she was his true love and bride-to-be, she was touched and delighted by Hugo Bauer's old-fashioned and unusual standards and feelings. They were very rare, virtually unique: indeed she had encountered such behavior only in certain films when her roles, as the heroine, had made her the young girl in a noble or a royal family.

In the interim before the celebration of the marriage, Hugo Bauer gazed in rapture and disbelief, each evening before he retired, at "The Heights of Joy," the film which had first made Magda Gehrhardt famous. It was a brilliant film, but it made her famous for the wrong reasons, because, in several episodes, Magda was entirely naked. Hugo Bauer watched the film each evening in solitude; he himself performed all the operations to project it upon his private screen because he wanted no one else to see it or to know that he gazed, with exaltation beyond belief, at his bride-to-be upon the screen, running in the woods, swimming in a forest pool on which the sunlight blazed in such a way that it was not certain at all times whether the image was that of shifting water or of the supple whiteness of Magda's body in the dazzle of the lake; emerging and running in the woods again and across a meadow and between trees, naked and self-delighted, her body almond white and sleek as a fawn, moving like a breaking wave, with the same grace, joy and spontaneity.

V

The marriage of Hugo Bauer and Magda Gehrhardt was celebrated with appropriate solemnity. The magnificence, however, was marred by an inevitable excess of publicity which Magda found distasteful. This distressed her even more than it distressed the bridegroom, perhaps because the nuptial occasion itself was so profoundly embarrassing to him. During the first weeks of the marriage, as the two travelled in the Mediterranean, it became clear to the financier that he was—as yet, at any rate— unable to achieve the kind of intimacy with his wife that he had known, although only briefly, with other women. He felt that this was his fault, some failing in him, some attitude of mind; for his bride was fine, generous, spontaneous, passionate and patient. He was now sure that she liked him very much for she gave herself to him with a grace and an innocence the existence of which he had never imagined; and which, had he imagined it, would have seemed to be possible only in a schoolgirl, not in a very beautiful and sophisticated film star.

He reflected often and with pain upon what was wrong, concealing his perplexity and brooding from his bride. After a time, it seemed to him very likely that she would remain, for him, an adored being, an idolized visual image: he was unable to move fully beyond the realm in which he gazed at her when he made love to her. This conclusion made him think once again of the time of adolescence when he had looked from a great distance upon a beautiful woman on the stage or upon the screen.

And this was the reason too that Hugo Bauer once

more sought the film in which he had seen his wife for the first time. He beheld "The Heights of Joy" once more, secretly and even furtively, amazed to discover what he had already suspected, that he found his wife as an image in a film far more exciting than the actuality he possessed so near him. Perhaps this state of mind would pass, after he had been married long enough, or become transformed, for the initial visual impression had been very powerful indeed: but a visual image, however dazzling, usually loses its power very soon. But as he thought of these possibilities, in the midst of beholding "The Heights of Joy," secretly, privately, and with deepening shame, for the first time since his marriage, Hugo was overtaken by the most cruel and painful of human emotions, a paralyzing jealousy of all other men who could look upon his wife in utter nakedness. Jealousy transformed "The Heights of Joy" into a hideous nightmare, a tormenting reminder of the complete and concrete reason for hatred. He switched off the current of power, rendering the screen blank, vague and empty, and an instant after he had expressed his anger by stopping the film in the midst of a scene, he determined to buy and destroy all copies of the film.

It was difficult for Hugo Bauer to look at his wife the next morning, for he was ashamed of the thoughts which had been the cause of so much torment throughout the sleepless night. He attempted to be sensible and rational about the jealousy he felt, telling himself that he possessed what other men desired: they were jealous of him and had no hope of possessing what he possessed: it was wholly irrational for him to be jealous of others who were jealous of him because of the same being. He also considered the probability that an effort to buy all the copies of "The Heights of Joy" would really reveal his own feelings of possessiveness and jealousy and shame. He would be the laughing stock of all those who knew about his feelings and the large expenditure of money he was willing to spend. There would be some who went to look at the film and stare at the star merely because they had heard of the financier's feelings.

By the end of the day, Hugo's sensible thoughts and resolutions collapsed, so great was the force of his resentment and jealousy, so overwhelming was his desire to prevent anyone else from beholding pictures of the nakedness of his wife. He would have liked very much, then, to consult Vincent De Vries, who so often had invaluable advice to give him and who was so much more of a man of the world. But Hugo was ashamed to speak of the matter with anyone, for his shame in having such feelings was surpassed only by the intensity with which these feelings possessed him.

Soon after, Hugo Bauer hired a private detective to act as his agent in securing all extant copies of the film which he had come, in a short time, to detest more than anything else in the world and which now inspired in him a passion like the desire for revenge. The detective could be trusted to keep the financier's confidence and his part in all transactions unknown. Since the detective was very capable, it was not long before Hugo Bauer began to receive copies of "The Heights of Joy" from all the great cities of Western and Central Europe. Upon receiving them, Bauer destroyed them quickly, using a chemical which dissolved celluloid film completely. He experienced a fury of hatred and delight as he watched the films dissolve into black fluids.

VI

All went well so far as securing those copies of "The Heights of Joy" that had remained in Europe. But within a month, the detective came to Hugo Bauer to report that it was far more difficult to deal with America and with the distributors of the film in America. In the New World, and particularly in the United States, it was necessary to avoid answering any question about why a copy of the film was being sought and why a large sum of money was being paid for it, for it was well-known, among distributors, that when "The Heights of Joy" had first been released, the usual number of copies had been distributed so that the film could be shown at the same time in the capitals of Europe. There had been an almost disastrous occurrence, which might have become public; it had been avoided only because the detective had discovered just in time that a European from whom copies of the film had been purchased had wired to America in an attempt to buy as many copies of the film as he could, doubtless hoping to be paid as much or more for them as he had already been paid for his own copies, perhaps guessing, since so much money was involved, that a very rich man's desires were the cause of the great expenditure of money.

Faced with this new difficulty, Hugo Bauer was reminded of like situations in matters of finance, in complicated deals when seeming disaster had been turned into triumph. Drawing upon his experience as a financier, Hugo Bauer moved immediately. He stopped all purchases of "The Heights of Joy," and offered through an intermediary to sell a great many copies: the market for copies collapsed overnight. The feeling that it was possible to make a killing by securing copies of the film had brought about a frantic quest and purchase of copies in America by this time, however. He decided that he would have to go to America himself: it was impossible to rely upon agents on the other side of the Atlantic, agents whom he did not know, whom he could not control, trust, or force to be discreet. Thus the quest, and the aim of annihilation of all copies of "The Heights of Joy" became international.

The entire transaction had so preoccupied Bauer that his attentions to his wife had diminished more than he was aware. And Magda, perceiving his absent-mindedness and accustomed, in any case, to infatuation, immediately became not only disturbed but so hurt that she suspected— unlikely as it seemed—that she had a rival: it would never have occurred to her that she was her own rival. It was useless for her to tell herself that once the first excitement ended an alteration and mellowing of feeling was inevitable in all marriages. She expected, as always, to fare far better than other women, and she always had until then.

Perplexed at first, and petulant after and finally disappointed and shocked in a new way, she was in an unsympathetic mood when her husband came to tell her that it would be necessary for him to go to America alone for at least a month. Again she suspected that her husband had fallen in love with another woman But she quickly realized that this could hardly be the reason for going to America: it was not even likely if the other woman were European, for a long ocean voyage would risk publicity far more than any other arrangement: and it was, in any case, not only unlike Hugo, but he did not seem to behave in the least like a human being in an amorous state, illicit or not. She remained hurt and inconsolable, however, for it was clear that Hugo was not telling her the truth when he said that he was going to America on a business matter which would be boring to hear about and which he could not tell her about, since it was a matter in which absolute confidence had been stipulated by others who were involved.

Perceiving the lack of conviction, the lack, even, of a simple plausibility of tone with which Hugo spoke, Magda misunderstood the reticence and again entertained the possibility of a serious rival. Consequently she herself was prey to notions of jealousy very much like those from which her husband had been suffering for some time, the very emotions which were driving him to cross the Atlantic to America to buy and destroy all the copies of "The Heights of Joy."

VII

During her husband's absence, Magda sought out Vincent De Vries, hoping to find out from him, however indirectly and tacitly, the reason for her husband's transatlantic voyage. She knew how intelligent Vincent was and how trusted. She did not know, nor could she have known, that "The Heights of Joy" was the only problem that Hugo had failed to confide in and to confer on with Vincent; the sole and absolute reason was his secret shame which he felt to be so much of a degradation because it was so much a matter of pure possessiveness, having no relation whatever to genuine jealousy, but arising from his helpless attachment to images and to an image.

While Hugo Bauer was in America, his wife and his secretary saw more of each other than they had until that time. Magda's quest for information about the cause of her husband's absence at first appeared to be authentic flirtation to Vincent De Vries, particularly since the actress, influenced to a great extent by the melodramatic and conspiratorial films in which she acted, used flirtation as a way of concealing the direction of her curiosity: thus she seemed somewhat like an international spy seeking to secure secrets of war from officers who belonged to the enemy's intelligence service.

When he recognized Magda's overtures as amorous, Vincent De Vries concealed his feelings and did not respond at all, pretending that he had not recognized them. He had long prided himself upon his foresight and prudence: he felt that any kind of behavior which risked his place and position of trust in relation to Hugo Bauer was certainly very foolish. And besides, there were many women who were all too willing to regard him with the utmost favor. Nevertheless, these thoughts existed at the top of his mind and exercised an influence upon only a part of his whole being: he too had been dazzled very much when he saw "The Heights of Joy," so that being alone with Magda renewed his sense of her radiant magnetism, and of how desirable she was. The day after it became clear that temptation was real, he sought to forestall the danger and keep it from becoming irresistible by resuming an old affair which had slowly come to an end the year before: his effort was useless, and for the first time he was willing to admit that all women were not at heart the same, or at least hardly different enough to justify the loss of some-thing more important by far, Hugo's friendship.

Magda's pursuit continued and she seemed to enjoy it merely as a pursuit, coming to his office unexpectedly when he was not prepared for her presence and thus inca-pable of concealing his true feelings immediately. Her feelings had been very much hurt, and the mystery of her husband's absence, his growing aloofness before his depar-ture and her sense of partial failure in not having sus-tained her husband's infatuation for very long—all combined to intensify her desires and her pursuit of her husband's best friend: Magda's pursuit was mocking in a way, and hence all the more difficult for Vincent De Vries to disregard. He wished that Hugo would return soon.

Thus it was that one evening after Hugo Bauer had been absent for little more than two weeks, Magda invited Vincent to dinner, an invitation too natural and ordinary to refuse. Soon after dinner—of which neither of them had eaten very much—Vincent and Magda found themselves locked in each other's arms before either knew for certain and with complete consciousness what was occurring, and certainly without any premeditation and conscious decision at a given moment on the part of either of them. At the last moment, when Magda perceived how nervous and distressed Vincent was, despite the fact that he was also overcome by desire, she attempted to put him at ease by declaring that no harm would be done and it would make no difference to Hugo so long as her husband remained ignorant of what had occurred: if he did not know, how could his feelings be hurt?

It was this which prevented Vincent De Vries from surrendering to the overwhelming immediacy of desire. For by giving Vincent a reason for not being nervous, she distracted him a little from the awareness of her offered beauty which had devoured his consciousness, made him sleepless, and driven all other things out of his mind. Her reason was weak—whether or not Hugo ever found out, he might be hurt, since Magda's attitude towards him would not be the same again—but the mere mention of a reason sufficed to restore Vincent De Vries to reason itself and to reasonable common sense, making him think of protecting himself from surrendering to a passing passion which would be the cause of harm to himself and to others. No one else might ever know, but he himself would know, his behavior toward Hugo would no longer be devoted and entirely candid, and worst of all, he would suffer from shame at being disloyal. Moreover, the more exalted the actual experience of making love to Magda was, the greater the frustration it would cause him thenceforth—since it could only be an episode, whatever Magda's intentions might be, and thus it might very well make his intimacy with other women far more unsatisfactory, just as other women were, to him, far less desirable—indeed they would become merely weak substitutes for Magda, if the experience of making love to her was all that he thought it must be.

After a brief effort at explanation and a brief apology in which Vincent included the truth that Magda loved her husband, he arose and departed, feeling that he had a dream of supreme fulfillment which, at its peak, suddenly had turned into a nightmare, an abyss of fear.

VIII

An ambitious and disappointed servant in Hugo Bauer's household wrote an anonymous note to Bauer, telling him that his wife had been unfaithful to him and that her lover was Vincent De Vries. The servant believed this to be the truth, although this was not what inspired him to write the anonymous note. Hugo had received anonymous notes before, and some of them had been attacks upon Vincent De Vries. He knew well enough that such letters were intended to injure himself or others, for the sake of personal gain or satisfaction of one or another kind. Hugo had reflected, at times, on the melodrama and the destructiveness to which power and wealth are prey and which are excited in other human beings who are close to power and wealth but do not possess them. Letters of this kind left him angry, but not for long, amused, or disgusted: but his behavior in responding to them was exactly the same as his behavior in response to most human actions: he considered, with care and patience, what it would be best to do for his own sake, setting his immediate emotions to one side and then dismissing them, concentrating upon his own welfare in the future, concentrating upon preventing it from being displeasing to him: he never felt there would be any good reason or benefit in punishing the wrongdoers whom the letter accused or the author of the letter.

This letter affected him very differently. It left him cool, curious and detached. He was naturally curious about the truth of the accusation, and detached because, as he suddenly saw, if the accusation were indeed true, which he doubted very much, he would be relieved of the exhausting and more and more humiliating, more and more degrading, consequences of his infatuation with his wife. It occurred to him instantly that if the accusation were true, he would no longer be the helpless victim of his desire to buy and destroy all the copies of "The Heights of Joy," a task that had become increasingly difficult and increasingly tedious as the value of each copy became known. Disloyalty and adultery would liberate him not only from "The Heights of Joy," but from the degrading, demoralizing emotions of jealousy and possessiveness. He knew now that he did not really want to be in love with his wife or any human being, to such an extent. It was a surrender of the self too great, too precarious, too barren and unsatisfactory: it made him cross oceans and visit another continent—merely for the sake of reels of celluloid containing images that had been seen many times by many human beings.

Hugo Bauer discovered, to his astonishment, that he was not hounded by the possibility of his wife's infidelity to any degree comparable to the hurt he had felt about "The Heights of Joy": it was necessary although painful to admit that his sense of possession, his feeling that what was his, should be by right denied to all others, had moved him far more than any other feeling. And now he felt almost terrified at the recognition of how blind love had rendered him, how overpowering and mutilating his love of his wife was: it was capable of making him foolish, and of exposing himself to the ridicule of millions, of devoting himself to a senseless quest in which his life became just as bewitched and monomaniacal, as passionate and as narrow, as the life of a gambler or a lyric poet.

It was no longer necessary, as a matter of the domination of emotion, to get hold of all the copies of "The Heights of Joy" in existence, whether or not the accusation was true. At a stroke, he was free, for the letter had made him see his own behavior and his own deepest motives clearly as if he judged the actions of another person.

Nevertheless, it was necessary as a matter of order and decorum, and adult manhood, to ascertain the truth about Magda and Vincent; and in any case, it would be an injustice to both of them and to himself to fail to make certain of the truth and live instead in a state of doubt and suspicion.

He decided to return to Paris immediately, by plane, and to arrive unannounced at an hour when a look into the faces of his wife and his friend would be sufficient to reveal whether they were guilty or innocent.

As his plane rose over the ground and over the Atlantic, Hugo Bauer felt that he was rising to a new kind of freedom.

But when he landed and went to his house, he was greeted by his wife with a warmth which seemed to reveal nothing whatever; her genuine fondness was unquestionable, whatever her fidelity, and her welcome might be innocence and fondness or guilt and expiation. Soon after, he summoned Vincent De Vries and since he felt he must conclude the matter soon by determining what the truth was, he said nothing to Vincent and when he saw no unequivocal evidence in Vincent's face, he showed him the anonymous note, remaining silent.

Vincent read the note, looked at Hugo Bauer, said nothing and left. Vincent De Vries felt that he was guilty of disloyalty and infidelity. Although nothing had occurred, if adultery was merely a physical actuality, desire had been so powerful—he had been locked in Magda's arms until the very last moment, all other feelings but desire having been vanished—hence Vincent felt that he was, in fact, guilty of adultery and of disloyalty.

Soon after, Vincent De Vries told Magda of the anonymous note and of his own sense of guilt, adding that he had been silent and that she was free to judge what had occurred without fearing any disclosure on his part. Magda felt far more guilty, for the same reasons as Vincent had felt guilt: she felt more guilty because she had courted Vincent and arranged a situation which he clearly wanted to avoid.

Both Vincent and Magda had the strange emotion—strange for them, at least—of being at once the victims of guilt and of frustration. Both had in their hearts been guilty of adultery and disloyalty and had incurred the most acute pain, while gaining none of the pleasure of making love, none of the gratification of great desire.

The silence of Magda and Vincent convinced Hugo Bauer that the accusation must be true. He felt an immense relief, as if a disease—the disease of love—had suddenly been banished and he had regained perfect health quickly. He was tempted to explain himself to Magda and Vincent, but he refrained, fearing that they would be offended or would not believe him.

Thenceforward all three were estranged, although they attempted in deference and in politeness and out of a sense of justice matched by a sense of guilt to continue life as if they were friends or belonged to the same family and had not seen one another for many years.

Vincent and Magda felt then that they had been

jilted or rejected by Hugo Bauer, and as a result each one's sense of guilt disappeared. The financier's impassive face expressed nothing but the absence of emotion. Magda felt, and said to herself, that the entire episode resembled the experience of regarding a film whose sound track has gone dead in the middle of a reel. Vincent De Vries felt that the experience was very much like that of coming to an unknown, strange and foreign city on a religious holiday when shops and streets are deserted. It also seemed to him like the encounter—or confrontation—of two human beings who have been accused of collaborating in a crime and who, when they meet, show no sign of having known each other before: there is no recognition in their faces, their response is trivial and pointless, and they are not sure whether or not they have committed the crime or merely dreamed about it, long ago.

IX

In a short time, the inevitable divorce of the financier and the film star became a legal actuality. The brevity of the marriage was the subject of comment in a good many publications. If no one had the least idea of what had happened, nevertheless the variety of speculations illustrated once again that error is inexhaustible, is infinite; while the truth is single and wholly concealed from a great many human beings, however curious and observant they may be.

It now became publicly known that Hugo Bauer had attempted to buy and destroy all the copies of "The Heights of Joy," but this fact, which appeared to be meaningless now that the financier and the film star were divorced, was more perplexing than revealing, particularly since the effort to get copies of the film had abruptly, ended. One curious observer guessed that there might be

some connection between their existence, which was inde-
structible, since new copies might always be made of "The
Heights of Joy," and the divorce which ended the brief
marriage. Yet this supposition explained nothing at all,
and it certainly did not reveal anything about the experiences and feelings of the married and divorced couple.

The author of the anonymous note remained as ambitious and as disappointed as he had been when he wrote
it. The financier, his friend, and the film star all prospered, each going in a different direction. Vincent De
Vries, with Hugo Bauer's help, secured a position superi-
or to and more lucrative than the one he had held with his
friend. Magda Gehrhardt accepted the invitation which
Hollywood had repeatedly and warmly sent her; she went
to America and to Hollywood and became famous as a
film star for a second time: she became an American film
star and played a heroine different indeed, after a time,
from her characteristic roles in Europe. Her films in
America were soon the direct cause of a new interest and
revival of her European films, and particularly of "The
Heights of Joy," which became extremely popular,
although it was cut a good deal. Magda married very soon
after becoming a successful Hollywood star: her new husband was a Hollywood director not unlike Hugo Bauer in
his concern with the power of wealth, for he was far more
interested in being certain that the films he directed were
box office successes than with their excellence as visual
narratives.

Hugo Bauer established many new enterprises in the
United States, Mexico and South America, feeling that he
no longer cared to restrict himself to Western Europe.
When he read the news of the second marriage of the wife
whom he had once adored with emotions so strong, so
strange and so obsessed, he felt at first disturbed, and the
pangs of jealousy recurred, as if he were still married to

Magda and he were gazing again at the nude sequences in "The Heights of Joy," alone in the dark of his projection room. He was, at this time, in Rio de Janiero, and he had with him, as it happened quite by accident, a copy of "The Heights of Joy." He hired what was necessary for a private showing of the film, and then, uneasy, troubled, uncertain, fearful of what his feelings would be, but believing that they would, at worst, merely be intensified for a brief period, he sat alone again in the dark of the hired projection room, managing the camera and other instruments with shaking, nervous hands.

But as the first reel began to glitter upon the screen, a calm and yet intoxicating pleasure—a serene exaltation—took hold of him: this began long before the reels containing the famous, or notorious, scenes, scenes in which his former wife, the very beautiful Magda Gehrhardt, ran, sauntered, swam, and laughed in the sunlight, on a midsummer afternoon, naked and radiant as the moonlight on a midsummer night, shining and distant and unattainable, in "The Heights of Joy."

The Statues

To MEYER SCHAPIRO

The snowfall began at five on the afternoon of the 8th of December. Faber Gottschalk, a dentist of thirty, walking to his office to meet one of his patients, was hardly aware of the first few feathers of snow. He had had a whiskey and soda but a moment before, and the pleasant bonfire liquor created in his whole being permitted him to think of the next hour without his customary distaste. Intimacy was what he resented most about his profession, the necessary acquaintance with the interior of the human mouth. To seek out decay, and pus, to do this day after day, to have this in the forefront of one's consciousness— these central aspects of his profession he disliked, did not get used to, and would never regard with anything but aversion. Consequently, as a habit of mind, he constantly evaded what immediately presented itself to him, the dinner he ate, the street on which he walked, or as on this afternoon, the first signs of the white whole and visual absolute of winter, the snow.

It was night before the sidewalks were covered over, and midnight before the remarkable character of the snow was evident. Hence, only the nightfolk, the police, the watchmen, the sleepless, and the drunken knew before morning that an extraordinary, inexplicable, and even terrifying event had occurred. Not only had the snowfall formed curious and unquestionable designs, some of which were very human; but also the snow had the hardness of rocks and could not be removed from the pavement.

The morning newspapers devoted three columns on the first page to this strange event. They commented especially on the difficulty of removing the snow, and printed photographs of the statues, as the snow objects were soon named. The photographs had been made before morning with the aid of flashes, and this heightened their uncanny and startling appearance.

Soon after, the newspapers of the late morning editions described the entire event as something quaint and full of human interest: there were stories of how different kinds of persons had responded to the whimsical and comical aspects of the snow, stories about the amazement of the housewife, the joy of the school children, and the inevitable fabulous lying of the old timers, who asserted that they had seen this sort of thing before, and in better style. Soon, however, this point of view was surrendered, because the entire populace was affected very differently by the statues. The stillness which comes with any great snow, the muffling and muting of sound, the slowing of pace and movement, the luxurious drag and trek of car and truck—these changes seemed to have entered into the very being of the citizens, so that they spoke slowly and softly, they moved serenely and as if soundlessly, they looked about with long stares, they looked about as if they were dream struck or abstracted or profoundly in love. The effect was much like that of a street-organ's operatic outburst, in which the music seems to take all the motions of the pedestrians into its flowing order.

Hence it was that the whole day after the snowfall became an unofficial holiday or fete. All private concerns were ignored, all tasks absentmindedly attended to, all other things put aside while everyone discussed, analyzed and sought an explanation of the remarkable statues of snow. The day was warm, sunny, and glittering, as often happens after a snowfall's catharsis, and the air was of a delightful purity and sweetness.

At noon the Mayor issued a statement to the press in which he promised that the snow would be removed as quickly as possible. This brought about the first example of the unanimity and intensity of feeling of the city, towards the statues. Everyone acted at once and in the same way precisely. The Mayor was overwhelmed by phone calls and even telegrams protesting against the removal of the snow. Even the Mayor's secretaries and assistants joined in exhorting him to do nothing about the snow, although some were anxious and unable to understand their emotions in this matter.

Faber Gottschalk, however, went even further. He attempted to visit City Hall, astonished at himself, unable to understand his passionate concern about the statues, but determined to do naught all day but walk about and look at them. Promised by the secretary of the Mayor that nothing would be done at present about removing the statues, he was left suspicious and unassured. No sooner had he left than he was disturbed by the ambiguous character of the phrase, "at present," saying to himself that that present was already past.

Faber Gottschalk cancelled all his appointments until further notice.

A mathematician at Columbia University, upon being interviewed, stated that the strange occurrence was proved by the laws of probability to be one which would probably have occurred, sooner or later.

Ministers of the various organized religions rewrote their sermons for the following Sunday, most of them adopting the view that the curious snowfall might be regarded as a literary allegory, so to speak. None of them ventured to suppose that any supernatural agency, divine or evil, was involved.

The children during the first day delighted in the comic strip surface of some of the statues, but soon some of them became annoyed that snowballs could not be fashioned out of the snow. In their frustration, they threw other available objects at each other, and one boy went so far as to open his brother's skull with a hockey stick.

Faber Gottschalk walked from the apartment which was both his home and his office to the Battery. Since this apartment was on Washington Heights, his walk was one of approximately ten miles, from one extreme to the other of Manhattan's long and narrow spine. Then he walked back again, surprised to find that the statues which studded his route disclosed new and even more interesting aspects when they were regarded for the second time. In fact, he attempted the experiment of circling a city block immediately after a second view of one statue, to see what new impression would occur. And there were new impressions, and they were very interesting, and it seemed to Faber Gottschalk that the statues had an inexhaustible nature.

By evening, he had returned to his apartment. Seated by his radio in the living room, he sought to understand the emotion which had overwhelmed him at the sight of the statues. As he reviewed the day in his mind, he smoked one cigar after another, gratified by the tobacco and yet able to distinguish clearly between the pleasure of smoking and the great happiness which had come upon him when he had awakened to see the strange snow things below his apartment window.

In seeking an explanation for his emotion, Faber Gottschalk thought of his past life, of the pattern, fate, or host of accidents which had brought him to this day. He had been persuaded to study dentistry by the uncle with whom he lived after his mother's death. His first ambition had been to be an athlete, and, failing in this, to be a sportswriter. Actually, he was not sure which of the two activities he desired more strongly. At any rate, the small complete world of the professional athlete interested him above all things, and since he had not the equipment to be very good at any sport, he had soon resigned himself without difficulty to being merely a spectator.

To be truly a spectator, however, is a great deal, for it involves the most intense partisanship, a life of the emotions which is at the mercy of success and defeat every day. In major league baseball, Faber's favorite sport, a fan follows the odyssey of his team for six months and more in every year, beginning with the spring training camps and culminating in the extraordinary excitement of the World Series. And this is a matter of a journey to eight cities, again and again, a trip which the fan endures in mind with no little anguish because it is more difficult for a team to win on a road trip than when playing before its own applauding audience.

Faber's uncle had pointed out to him that as a dentist he would have a modest income, and he would be able to arrange his hours of work in such a way as to permit him to follow the sports which absorbed his free attention through the year. Faber had no reason to regret the fact that he had acted on his uncle's counsel. He had arrived at the age of thirty, moved by the profound disgust with his profession which has already been noted, but he had been free to develop and satisfy the habits and appetites of a spectator. Although he felt that his life was a might-as-well matter, he had no reason to suppose it might have been better, if he had striven more.

During the long evening, seated in the darkness of the living room and going to the window from time to time to look down at the city street where the figures lay, blue-white and ghastly like shrouded corpses, Faber Gottschalk was unable to explain to himself by his examination of his past life the reason for his emotion about the statues.

The huge event was succeeded by a week of perfect weather. The snow did not melt, nor did the statues alter. They remained firmly attached to the pavement as if they were a natural outgrowth of the asphalt, and automobiles found it necessary to move circumspectly and circuitously about them.

When the newspapers had exhausted all the approaches to the subject of which they were capable, when thousands had come from suburb and distant city to see the new sights, and then remained, unable to depart, fascinated and obsessed, then a broad and sharp change took place in the consciousness of the populace, among the rich and the poor, the middle-class and the working-class. During the day, many would go to the window to look down at the statues, and many during the lunch hour would eat hurriedly or would not eat at all or would munch sandwiches in the street that they might be able to look longer at the creations of the fall. The strikes which occurred at this time continued without abatement, but the pickets were often absorbed in the figures outstretched upon the white ground; and in this contemplation, in this absorption, they were often joined by the police, who, despite this unity of interests, did not cease to check them. Even a boss at times would pass, pause to look at the statues, then look up again at the pickets with undisguised hatred. In general, everyone did what he was expected to do, but in a new way, with more concentration, with more devotion, and more efficiently. At certain moments, everything stopped and was motionless, as at a red light on a great avenue; and in this motionless period, complete attention was given to the statues, as when a noble man's death is regarded.

From each borough of the city of New York came news of the variety of the statues, and reports of the absorption of the citizens in the statues, an absorption which seemed to rise above the habits and acts of daily existence, but not to destroy them. Faber Gottschalk alone surrendered the being of his past life utterly, ceased to practise his profession, and went through the conscious day throughout New York in an effort to see all the statues.

Many of these statues were grotesque. Some were monstrous. Some resembled human figures, and although they were of a perfect verisimilitude in all else, the faces were at times blank as a plate, distorted like gargoyles, or obscene, as when, in certain suburbs, figures clung to each other in an embrace which was hardly ambiguous. Elsewhere, however, the statues had the rotundity and the plumpness of the cumulus clouds of a summer's day, the solidity and the stillness of fine buildings, or the pure and easy design of some flowers. Everywhere were forms which delighted the eye either as fresh complexes of previously known designs, or compositions which seemed to exhaust the possibility of arrangement. The populace's fondness for the statues continually increased, and soon many of them were given nicknames: one was called "Versailles," because of its glitter in the sunlight, like light shining upon many mirrors; one, a great gross one, was named, "Caliban"; then there were such names as "Sky Folly," "Sestina," "Chios," "Hallucination," "Plum Elected," "Old Nick" and "Shelley."

In certain quarters, and indeed everywhere at times, there occurred much speculation as to the source, sources, cause or causes of the phenomenal snow. Soon it was decided that the entire system of the snow had been a wonderful chance like perfect weather or a rockface. Some for a time spoke of the fecundity of nature; some—these were the ones who were often alone—thought that this was indeed the way that the haunted and hunted lives of human beings took shape by an unpredictable and continuous fall to which little or no designing agency could be attributed.

Slowly, after much thought, waking from troubled sleep, or pausing on a stair, Faber Gottschalk recognized that for him, at least for him, these wonderful objects were of such grave interest because they resembled the white teeth which were, so to speak, the subject-matter of his profession. But, recognizing this, he was merely confronted with a greater degree of perplexity. Why should he take such delight in the statues, since teeth were an abomination to him?

At art galleries and theatres attendances became meager. The chief attraction at the moving picture houses was the newsreel in which it was possible to see figures which were in other distant parts of the city. The audiences at these newsreels regarded the statues with an interest which was equalled by their interest in the attitudes and emotions of citizens photographed in the act of looking at the statues. (Here we must presume that it is possible to draw a valid distinction between the interest in the statues and the interest in the spectators, for they were always part of one scene.)

No one laughed at the rapt expressions on the faces of some spectators (they were, the audience, too enraptured themselves), nor at the old men who seemed to become statues too, as they stood in stillness staring at the statues. But one audience did become very angry when a boy of thirteen was shown in the act of drawing a mustache on one of the figures' faces. Apart from this resentment of any act of change, the audience were of a pure seriousness as they gazed in the darkness at the screen. And one woman broke into tears when she saw a crowd of men standing before a statue and looking at it as if they regarded Niagara Falls.

Bars, restaurants, theatres, and museums lost a great deal of patronage. And yet those most directly concerned, the owners and the managers, did not seem at all troubled. Perhaps this was because of the general and indeed unanimous feeling that all was well, at least for the time being.

Yet, if many of the figures were of a matchless beauty, there was one which, as a literal thing, was so shocking, so appalling, and outrageous, that certain citizens petitioned the mayor to the effect that it be removed at once, by dynamite. This was the cause of one harsh conflict of this period of good feeling, for overflowing crowds, hearing of the petition, protested immediately, demanding that nothing be done. The sentiment thus became explicit and conscious that every object of the wondrous fall was somehow of a perfect preciousness and importance, and must be guarded with the utmost care, preserved at all costs, and never destroyed. Faber Gottschalk hearing of the petition a little late, came hurrying to the scene, the most avid advocate of the preservation of the statue.

III

On a street corner, near a lamp-post, standing on the rumbleseat of a motor car, he harangued a crowd which was decidedly in agreement with him. As he neared the end of his speech and sought a certain conclusiveness or resolution, he was troubled by the sense that he himself did not truly understand what he was saying.

"So I say to you," he said, "there is every reason to believe we have no right to modify any of these new

97

things. Those who have been in favor of getting rid of this statue, which they avow to be obscene, tell us that the children will be corrupted by it. I will not say in reply that we cannot permit our lives to be determined by what the children will or will not see. Such an answer would be too easy, although true enough. I will not advance the argument that those of us who really know children and have lived with them know very well that it is the children, not the adults, nor the statues, who are corrupt, whence it is that our adult lives are a long suffering and chiefly unsuccessful attempt to free ourselves from the utter corruption of childhood, infancy, and the egotism contracted in the womb. I myself remember very well, how at the age of eight, on a visit at my aunt's, my two female cousins, twins, took me into the closet and taught me certain things of which I must already have been somewhat aware, because I was scarcely surprised by what they did to me.

"But apart from these considerations, and apart from the children, who can be trusted, I assure you, to take care of themselves, I want to impress upon or rather recall to you something on which we are certainly in some sense agreed—"

(Here the speaker showed his hesitancy most of all.)

"To anything which is beautiful, to anything which is true, to anything which is good we are committed, though the commitment jeopardizes our lives. Further-more—"

(This last word bore in tone the lack of conviction felt by the speaker.)

"—since we really do not understand these extraordinary objects, must we not, from motives of humility, prudence, and practicality, regard them as sacred mysteries, at least for the time being? Who knows what relationship they may not have to our lives? What natural or supernatural powers may not, through them, be signing to us? Do any of you have the presumption and insensitivity to maintain that you do not know more and honor more in the nature of things than you did at the age of fifteen?—"

Few understood the latter remark, but the crowd cheered Faber vehemently as he dismounted from the car. They liked his tone and they were in favor of his emotion. When one listener, an intellectual, sought Faber out in the bar of a nearby restaurant, he was at first merely interested in repeating what he had just said, and emphasizing again and again the close relationship he felt between teeth, sports, and statues. Some peculiar and necessary importance seemed to be involved in their connection.

When Faber's questioner kindly suggested to him that he ought not to permit this passion to disrupt his life, since there were, after all, other important and necessary things, Faber replied: "If one becomes sufficiently interested, wholly absorbed, and absolutely involved in any one thing, or any passion, then that thing or that passion becomes the whole world for one, the whole world appears once more in it, and with more intensity and clarity. The same difficulties, the same duties and necessities reappear, translated into the terms of this purely important thing. For if one becomes completely interested in any thing, it ceases to be a thing among other things, it ceases to be a thing in essence, it becomes the whole world."

Seldom have the mouths of dentists uttered sentiments so serious and metaphysical.

Gottschalk's speech and the solidarity of other like-minded persons won out, and the obscene statue was left intact. The enchantment which had made New York a sleep-walking city of contemplatives continued with no diminution of attention. At the conclusion of the tenth day of the presence of the statues, a period of unblemished weather, it was felt by many that these marble white beauties were permanent parts of the city. The gross figure resembling a giant pharoah which had descended upon an Elevated station was washed clean by a troop of painstaking Elevated passengers, after the soot of the city had darkened it. Like acts of pious ablution were performed all over, which seemed to show through this unanimity of feeling a new kind of *Burggeist*.

And then, without warning, a tireless and foul rain descended and to everyone's surprise utterly destroyed the fine statues. Their disappearance was noted on the first page of the next morning's newspapers, but not in the headlines, as with their arrival. Everyone resumed the customary problems, old enmities were revived as if they had not been interrupted, as if their continuance had not been lifted to a new level for a time; and immediately the motion-picture theatres, theatres, libraries, and galleries enjoyed a sudden flood of patrons.

A particularly brutal murder was committed in Brooklyn, the sport pages carried much news about ice sports at winter resorts, a boy of seventeen, scion of a very rich family, disappeared from his home and was found only after two weeks in Iceland, Faber Gottschalk jumped or fell in front of an onrushing subway train, and only a few were sufficiently disturbed to keep in mind, with the help of photographs, the holy time when statues had presented their marvellous forms everywhere in the city of New York.

At a Solemn Musick

Let the musicians begin,
Let every instrument awaken and instruct us
In love's willing river and love's dear discipline:
We wait, silent, in consent and in the penance
Of patience, awaiting the serene exaltation
Which is the liberation and conclusion of expiation.

Now may the chief musician say:
"Lust and emulation have dwelt among us
Like barbarous kings: have conquered us:
Have inhabited our hearts: devoured and ravished
—With the savage greed and avarice of fire—
The substance of pity and compassion."

Now may all the players play:
"The river of the morning, the morning of the river
Flow out of the splendor of the tenderness of surrender."

Now may the chief musician say:
"Nothing is more important than summer."

And now the entire choir shall chant:
"How often the astonished heart,
Beholding the laurel,
Remembers the dead,
And the enchanted absolute,
Snow's kingdom, sleep's dominion."

Then shall the chief musician declare:

"The phoenix is the meaning of the fruit,
Until the dream is knowledge and knowledge is a dream."

And then, once again the entire choir shall cry,
                           in passionate unity,
Singing and celebrating love and love's victory,
Ascending and descending the heights of assent,
                 climbing and chanting triumphantly:
Before the morning was, you were:
Before the snow shone,
And the light sang, and the stone,
Abiding, rode the fullness or endured the emptiness,
You were: you were alone.

Tired and Unhappy, You Think of Houses

Tired and unhappy, you think of houses
Soft-carpeted and warm in the December evening,
While snow's white pieces fall past the window,
And the orange firelight leaps.
                       A young girl sings
That song of Gluck where Orpheus pleads with
                                 Death;
Her elders watch, nodding their happiness
To see time fresh again in her self-conscious eyes:
The servants bring the coffee, the children retire,
Elder and younger yawn and go to bed,
The coals fade and glow, rose and ashen,
It is time to shake yourself! and break this
Banal dream, and turn your head
Where the underground is charged, where the weight
Of the lean buildings is seen,

Where close in the subway rush, anonymous
In the audience, well-dressed or mean,
So many surround you, ringing your fate,
Caught in an anger exact as a machine!

Darkling Summer,
Ominous Dusk, Rumorous Rain

1

A tattering of rain and then the reign
Of pour and pouring-down and down,
Where in the westward gathered the filming gown
Of grey and clouding weakness, and, in the mane
Of the light's glory and the day's splendor, gold and vain,
Vivid, more and more vivid, scarlet, lucid and more
                                        luminous,
Then came a splatter, a prattle, a blowing rain!
And soon the hour was musical and rumorous:
A softness of a dripping lipped the isolated houses,
A gaunt grey somber softness licked the glass of hours.

2

Again, after a catbird squeaked in the special silence,
And clouding vagueness fogged the windowpane
And gathered blackness and overcast, the mane
Of light's story and light's glory surrendered and ended
—A pebble—a ring—a ringing on the pane,
A blowing and a blowing in: tides of the blue and cold
Moods of the great blue bay, and slates of grey
Came down upon the land's great sea, the body of this day
—Hardly an atom of silence amid the roar
Allowed the voice to form appeal—to call:
By kindled light we thought we saw the bronze of fall.

Spiders

Is the spider a monster in miniature?
His web is a cruel stair, to be sure,
Designed artfully, cunningly placed,
A delicate trap, carefully spun
To bind the fly (innocent or unaware)
In a net as strong as a chain or a gun.

There are far more spiders than the man in the street
supposes
And the philosopher-king imagines, let alone knows!
There are six hundred kinds of spiders and each one
Differs in kind and in unkindness.
In variety of behavior spiders are unrivalled:
The fat garden spider sits motionless, amidst or at the
heart
Of the orb of its web: other kinds run,
Scuttling across the floor, falling into bathtubs,
Trapped in the path of its own wrath, by overconfidence
drowned and undone.

Other kinds—more and more kinds under the stars and
the sun—
Are carnivores: all are relentless, ruthless
Enemies of insects. Their methods of getting food
Are unconventional, numerous, various and sometimes
hilarious:
Some spiders spin webs as beautiful
As Japanese drawings, intricate as clocks, strong as rocks:
Others construct traps which consist only

Of two sticky and tricky threads. Yet this ambush is
                                                    enough
To bind and chain a crawling ant for long enough:
The famished spider feels the vibration
Which transforms patience into sensation and satiation.
The handsome wolf spider moves suddenly freely and relies
Upon lightning suddenness, stealth and surprise,
Possessing accurate eyes, pouncing upon his victim with
                                    the speed of surmise.

Courtship is dangerous: there are just as many elaborate
                            and endless techniques and varieties
As characterize the wooing of more analytic, more intro-
                            spective beings: Sometimes the male
Arrives with the gift of a freshly caught fly.
Sometimes he ties down the female, when she is frail,
With deft strokes and quick maneuvres and threads of silk:
But courtship and wooing, whatever their form, are
                                                    informed
By extreme caution, prudence, and calculation,
For the female spider, lazier and fiercer than the male
                                                    suitor,
May make a meal of him if she does not feel in the same
                            mood, or if her appetite
Consumes her far more than the revelation of love's
                                            consummation.
Here among spiders, as in the higher forms of nature,
The male runs a terrifying risk when he goes seeking for
                the bounty of beautiful Alma Magna Mater:
Yet clearly and truly he must seek and find his mate and
                match like every other living creature!

Father and Son

"From a certain point onward there is no longer any turning back. That is the point that must be reached."
—FRANZ KAFKA

Father:
On these occasions, the feelings surprise,
Spontaneous as rain, and they compel
Explicitness, embarrassed eyes—

Son:
Father, you're not Polonius, you're reticent,
But sure. I can already tell
The unction and falsetto of the sentiment
Which gratifies the facile mouth, but springs
From no felt, had, and wholly known things.

Father:
You must let me tell you what you fear
When you wake up from sleep, still drunk with sleep:
You are afraid of time and its slow drip,
Like melting ice, like smoke upon the air
In February's glittering sunny day.
Your guilt is nameless, because its name is time,
Because its name is death. But you can stop
Time as it dribbles from you, drop by drop.

Son:
But I thought time was full of promises,
Even as now, the emotion of going away—

Father:

That is the first of all its menaces,
The lure of a future different from today;
All of us always are turning away
To the cinema and Asia. All of us go
To one indeterminate nothing.

Son:

Must it be so?
I question the sentiment you give to me,
As premature, not to be given, learned alone
When experience shrinks upon the chilling bone.
I would be sudden now and rash in joy,
As if I lived forever, the future my toy.
Time is a dancing fire at twenty-one,
Singing and shouting and drinking to the sun,
Powerful at the wheel of a motor-car,
Not thinking of death which is foreign and far.

Father:

If time flowed from your will and were a feast
I would be wrong to question your zest.
But each age betrays the same weak shape.
Each moment is dying. You will try to escape
From melting time and your dissipating soul
By hiding your head in a warm and dark hole.
See the evasions which so many don,
To flee the guilt of time they become one,
That is, the one number among masses,
The one anonymous in the audience,
The one expressionless in the subway,
In the subway evening among so many faces,
The one who reads the daily newspaper,
Separate from actor and act, a member
Of public opinion, never involved.

Integrated in the revery of a fine cigar,
Fleeing to childhood at the symphony concert,
Buying sleep at the drugstore, grandeur
At the band concert, Hawaii
On the screen, and everywhere a specious splendor:
One, when he is sad, has something to eat,
An ice cream soda, a toasted sandwich,
Or has his teeth fixed, but can always retreat
From the actual pain, and dream of the rich.
This is what one does, what one becomes
Because one is afraid to be alone,
Each with his own death in the lonely room.
But there is a stay. You can stop
Time as it dribbles from you, drop by drop.

Son:
Now I am afraid. What is there to be known?

Father:
Guilt, guilt of time, nameless guilt.
Grasp firmly your fear, thus grasping your self,
Your actual will. Stand in mastery,
Keeping time in you, its terrifying mystery.
Face yourself, constantly go back
To what you were, your own history.
You are always in debt. Do not forget
The dream postponed which would not quickly get
Pleasure immediate as drink, but takes
The travail, of building, patience with means.
See the wart on your face and on your friend's face,
On your friend's face and indeed on your own face.
The loveliest woman sweats, the animal stains
The ideal which is with us like the sky . . .

Son:
Because of that, some laugh, and others cry.

Father:
Do not look past and turn away your face.
You cannot depart and take another name,
Nor go to sleep with lies. Always the same,
Always the same self from the ashes of sleep
Returns with its memories, always, always,
The phoenix with eight hundred thousand memories!

Son:
What must I do that is most difficult?

Father:
You must meet your death face to face,
You must, like one in an old play,
Decide, once for all, your heart's place.
Love, power, and fame stand on an absolute
Under the formless night and the brilliant day,
The searching violin, the piercing flute.
Absolute! Venus and Caesar fade at that edge,
Hanging from the fiftieth-story ledge,
Or diminished in bed when the nurse presses
Her sickening unguents and her cold compresses.
When the news is certain, surpassing fear,
You touch the wound, the priceless, the most dear.
There in death's shadow, you comprehend
The irreducible wish, world without end.

Son:
I begin to understand the reason for evasion,
I cannot partake of your difficult vision.

Father:
Begin to understand the first decision.
Hamlet is the example; only dying
Did he take up his manhood, the dead's burden,
Done with evasion, done with sighing,
Done with revery.
                    Decide that you are dying
Because time is in you, ineluctable
As shadow, named by no syllable.
Act in that shadow, as if death were now:
Your own self acts then, then you know.

Son:
My father has taught me to be serious.

Father:
Be guilty of yourself in the full looking-glass.

Far Rockaway

"the cure of souls."—HENRY JAMES

The radiant soda of the seashore fashions
Fun, foam, and freedom. The sea laves
The shaven sand. And the light sways forward
On the self-destroying waves.

The rigor of the weekday is cast aside with shoes,
With business suits and the traffic's motion;
The lolling man lies with the passionate sun,
Or is drunken in the ocean.

A socialist health takes hold of the adult,
He is stripped of his class in the bathing-suit,
He returns to the children digging at summer,
A melon-like fruit.

O glittering and rocking and bursting and blue
—Eternities of sea and sky shadow no pleasure:
Time unheard moves and the heart of man is eaten
Consummately at leisure.

The novelist tangential on the boardwalk overhead
Seeks his cure of souls in his own anxious gaze.
"Here," he says, "With whom?" he asks, 'This?" he
                                                questions,
"What tedium, what blaze?"

"What satisfaction, fruit? What transit, heaven?

Criminal? justified? arrived at what June?"
That nervous conscience amid the concessions
Is a haunting, haunted moon.

Starlight Like Intuition
Pierced the Twelve

The starlight's intuitions pierced the twelve,
The brittle night sky sparkled like a tune
Tinkled and tapped out on the xylophone.
Empty and vain, a glittering dune, the moon
Arose too big, and, in the mood which ruled,
Seemed like a useless beauty in a pit;
And then one said, after he carefully spat:
"No matter what we do, he looks at it!

"I cannot see a child or find a girl
Beyond his smile which glows like that spring moon."
"—Nothing no more the same," the second said,
"Though all may be forgiven, never quite healed
The wound I bear as witness, standing by;
No ceremony surely appropriate,
Nor secret love, escape or sleep because
No matter what I do, he looks at it—"

"Now," said the third, "no thing will be the same:
I am as one who never shuts his eyes,
The sea and sky no more are marvellous,
And I no longer understand surprise!"
"Now," said the fourth, "nothing will be enough
—I heard his voice accomplishing all wit:
No word can be unsaid, no deed withdrawn
—No matter what is said, he measures it!"

"Vision, imagination, hope or dream,
Believed, denied, the scene we wished to see?
It does not matter in the least: for what
Is altered, if it is not true? That we
Saw goodness, as it is—*this* is the awe
And the abyss which we will not forget,
His story now the sky which holds all thought:
No matter what I think, think of it!"

"And I will never be what once I was,"
Said one for long as narrow as a knife,
"And we will never be what once we were;
We have died once, this is a second life."
"My mind is spilled in moral chaos," one
Righteous as Job exclaimed, "now infinite
Suspicion of my heart stems what I will
—No matter what I choose, he stares at it!"

"I am as one native in summer places
—Ten weeks' excitement paid for by the rich;
Debauched by that and then all winter bored,"
The sixth declared. "His peak left us a ditch!"
"He came to make this life more difficult,"
The seventh said, "No one will ever fit
His measure's heights, all is inadequate:
No matter what I do, what good is it?"

"He gave forgiveness to us: what a gift!"
The eighth chimed in. "But now we know how much
Must be forgiven. But if forgiven, what?
The crime which was will be; and the least touch
Revives the memory: what is forgiveness worth?"
The ninth spoke thus: "Who now will ever sit
At ease in Zion at the Easter feast?
No matter what the place, he touches it!"

"And I will always stammer, since he spoke,"
One, who had been most eloquent, said, stammering.
"I looked too long at the sun; like too much light,
So too much goodness is a boomerang,"
Laughed the eleventh of the troop. "I must
Try what he tried: I saw the infinite
Who walked the lake and raised the hopeless dead:
No matter what the feat, he first accomplished it!"

So spoke the twelfth; and then the twelve in chorus:
"Unspeakable unnatural goodness is
Risen and shines, and never will ignore us;
He glows forever in all consciousness;
Forgiveness, love, and hope possess the pit
And bring our endless guilt, like shadow's bars:
No matter what we do, he stares at it!

What pity then deny? what debt defer?
We know he looks at us like all the stars,
And we shall never be as once we were,
This life will never be what once it was!"

"I am Cherry Alive," the Little Girl Sang

For MISS KATHLEEN HANLON

"I am cherry alive," the little girl sang,
"Each morning I am something new:
I am apple, I am plum, I am just as excited
As the boys who made the Hallowe'en bang:
I am tree, I am cat, I am blossom too:
When I like, if I like, I can be someone new,
Someone very old, a witch in a zoo:

I can be someone else whenever I think who,
And I want to be everything sometimes too:
And the peach has a pit and I know that too,
And I put it in along with everything
To make the grown-ups laugh whenever I sing:
And I sing: *It is true; It is untrue;*
I know, I know, the true is untrue,
The peach has a pit, the pit has a peach:
And both may be wrong when I sing my song,
But I don't tell the grown-ups: because it is sad,
And I want them to laugh just like I do
Because they grew up and forgot what they knew
And they are sure I will forget it some day too.
They are wrong. They are wrong. When I sang my
                                song, I knew, I knew!
I am red, I am gold, I am green, I am blue,
I will always be me, I will always be new!"

The Heavy Bear Who Goes With Me
'the withness of the body'

The heavy bear who goes with me,
A manifold honey to smear his face,
Clumsy and lumbering here and there,
The central ton of every place,
The hungry beating brutish one
In love with candy, anger, and sleep,
Crazy factotum, dishevelling all,
Climbs the building, kicks the football,
Boxes his brother in the hate-ridden city.

Breathing at my side, that heavy animal,
That heavy bear who sleeps with me,

Howls in his sleep for a world of sugar,
A sweetness intimate as the water's clasp,
Howls in his sleep because the tight-rope
Trembles and shows the darkness beneath.
—The strutting show-off is terrified,
Dressed in his dress-suit, bulging his pants,
Trembles to think that his quivering meat
Must finally wince to nothing at all.

That inescapable animal walks with me,
Has followed me since the black womb held,
Moves where I move, distorting my gesture,
A caricature, a swollen shadow,
A stupid clown of the spirit's motive,
Perplexes and affronts with his own darkness,
The secret life of belly and bone,
Opaque, too near, my private, yet unknown,
Stretches to embrace the very dear
With whom I would walk without him near,
Touches her grossly, although a word
Would bare my heart and make me clear,
Stumbles, flounders, and strives to be fed
Dragging me with him in his mouthing care,
Amid the hundred million of his kind,
The scrimmage of appetite everywhere.

Sonnet:
O City, City

To live between terms, to live where death
Has his loud picture in the subway ride,
Being amid six million souls, their breath
An empty song suppressed on every side,
Where the sliding auto's catastrophe
Is a gust past the curb, where numb and high
The office building rises to its tyranny,
Is our anguished diminution until we die.

Whence, if ever, shall come the actuality
Of a voice speaking the mind's knowing
The sunlight bright on the green windowshade,
And the self articulate, affectionate, and flowing,
Ease, warmth, light, the utter showing,
When in the white bed all things are made.

Lincoln

Manic-depressive Lincoln, national hero!
How just and true that this great nation, being conceived
In liberty by fugitives should find
—Strange ways and plays of monstrous History—
This Hamlet-type to be the President—

This failure, this unwilling bridegroom,
This tricky lawyer full of black despair—

He grew a beard, becoming President,
And took a shawl as if he guessed his role,
Though with the beard he fled cartoonists' blacks,
And many laughed and were contemptuous,
And some for four years spoke of killing him—

He was a politician—of the heart!—
He lived from hand to mouth in moral things!
He understood quite well Grant's drunkenness!
It was for him, before Election Day,
That at Cold Harbor Grant threw lives away
In hopeless frontal attack against Lee's breastworks!

O how he was the Hamlet-man, and this,
After a life of failure made him right,
After he ran away on his wedding day,
Writing a coward's letter to his bride—
How with his very failure, he out-tricked
The florid Douglas and the abstract Davis,
And all the vain men who, surrounding him,
Smiled in their vanity and sought his place—

Later, they made him out a prairie Christ
To sate the need coarse in the national heart—

His wife went insane, Mary Todd too often
Bought herself dresses. And his child died.
And he would not condemn young men to death
For having slept, in weakness. And he spoke
More than he knew and all that he had felt
Between outrageous joy and black despair
Before and after Gettysburg's pure peak—

He studied law, but knew in his own soul
Despair's anarchy, terror and error,

—Instruments had to be taken from his office
And from his bedroom in such days of horror,
Because some saw that he might kill himself:
When he was young, when he was middle-aged,
How just and true was he, our national hero!

Sometimes he could not go home to face his wife,
Sometimes he wished to hurry or end his life!
But do not be deceived. He did not win,
And, it is plain, the South could never win
(Despite the gifted Northern generals!)
—Capitalismus is not mocked, O no!
This stupid deity decided the War—

In fact, the North and South were losers both:
—Capitalismus won the Civil War—

—Capitalismus won the Civil War,
Yet, in the War's cruel Colosseum,
Some characters fulfilled their natures' surds,
Grant the drunkard, Lee the noble soldier,
John Brown in whom the Bible soared and cried,
Booth the unsuccessful Shakespearean,
—Each in some freedom walked and knew himself,
Then most of all when all the deities
Mixed with their barbarous stupidity
To make the rock, root, and rot of the war—

"This is the way each only life becomes,
Tossed on History's ceaseless insane sums!"

Seurat's Sunday Afternoon Along the Seine

To MEYER AND LILLIAN SCHAPIRO

What are they looking at? Is it the river?
The sunlight on the river, the summer, leisure,
Or the luxury and nothingness of consciousness?
A little girl skips, a ring-tailed monkey hops
Like a kangaroo, held by a lady's lead
(Does the husband tax the Congo for the monkey's keep?)
The hopping monkey cannot follow the poodle dashing
ahead.

Everyone holds his heart within his hands:

A prayer, a pledge of grace or gratitude
A devout offering to the god of summer, Sunday and
plenitude.

The Sunday people are looking at hope itself.

They are looking at hope itself, under the sun, free from
the teething anxiety, the gnawing nervousness
Which wastes so many days and years of consciousness.

The one who beholds them, beholding the gold and green
Of summer's Sunday is himself unseen. This is because
he is
Dedicated radiance, supreme concentration, fanatically
threading
The beads, needles and eyes—at once!—of vividness
and permanence.

He is a saint of Sunday in the open air, a fanatic
                                        disciplined
By passion, courage, passion, skill, compassion, love:
            the love of life and the love of light as one,
                under the sun, with the love of life.

Everywhere radiance glows like a garden in stillness
                                        blossoming.

Many are looking, many are holding something or
                                        someone
Little or big: some hold several kinds of parasols:
Each one who holds an umbrella holds it differently
One hunches under his red umbrella as if he hid
And looked forth at the river secretly, or sought to be
Free of all of the others' judgement and proximity.
Next to him sits a lady who has turned to stone, or
                                become a boulder,
Although her bell-and-sash hat is red.
A little girl holds to her mother's arm
As if it were a permanent genuine certainty:
Her broad-brimmed hat is blue and white, blue like the
                                river, like the sailboats white,
And her face and her look have all the bland innocence,
Open and far from fear as cherubims playing harpsichords.
An adolescent girl holds a bouquet of flowers
As if she gazed and sought her unknown, hoped-for,
                                        dreaded destiny.
No hold is as strong as the strength with which the trees,
Grip the ground, curve up to the light, abide in the
                                        warm kind air:
Rooted and rising with a perfected tenacity
Beyond the distracted erratic case of mankind there.
Every umbrella curves and becomes a tree,
And the trees curving, arise to become and be

Like the umbrella, the bells of Sunday, summer, and
                                        Sunday's luxury.
Assured as the trees is the strolling dignity
Of the bourgeois wife who holds her husband's arm
With the easy confidence and pride of one who is
—She is sure—a sovereign Victorian empress and
                                        queen.
Her husband's dignity is as solid as his *embonpoint*:
He holds a good cigar, and a dainty cane, quite
                                        carelessly.
He is held by his wife, they are each other's property,
Dressed quietly and impeccably, they are suave and
                                        grave
As if they were unaware or free of time, and the grave,
Master and mistress of Sunday's promenade—of
                                        everything!
 —As they are absolute monarchs of the ring-tailed
                                        monkey.
If you look long enough at anything
It will become extremely interesting;
If you look very long at anything
It will become rich, manifold, fascinating:

If you can look at any thing for long enough,
You will rejoice in the miracle of love,
You will possess and be blessed by the marvellous
            blinding radiance of love, you will be radiance.
Selfhood will possess and be possessed, as in the
        consecration of marriage, the mastery of vocation, the
            mystery of gift's mastery, the deathless relation of
                                        parenthood and progeny.
All things are fixed in one direction:
We move with the Sunday people from right to left.

The sun shines

122

In soft glory
Mankind finds
The famous story
Of peace and rest, released for a little while from the
          tides of weekday tiredness, the grinding anxiousness
Of daily weeklong lifelong fear and insecurity,
The profound nervousness which in the depths of
                              consciousness
Gnaws at the roots of the teeth of being so continually,
                    whether in sleep or wakefulness,
We are hardly aware that it is there or that we might
                              ever be free
Of its ache and torment, free and open to all experience.

The Sunday summer sun shines equally and voluptuously
Upon the rich and the free, the comfortable, the *rentier*,
          the poor, and those who are paralyzed by poverty.
Seurat is at once painter, poet, architect, and alchemist:
The alchemist points his magical wand to describe and
                    hold the Sunday's gold,
Mixing his small alloys for long and long
Because he wants to hold the warm leisure and pleasure
                              of the holiday
Within the fiery blaze and passionate patience of his
                              gaze and mind
Now and forever: O happy, happy throng,
it is forever Sunday, summer, free: you are forever warm
Within his little seeds, his small black grains,
He builds and holds the power and the luxury
With which the summer Sunday serenely reigns.

—Is it possible? It is possible!—
Although it requires the labors of Hercules, Sisyphus,
                              Flaubert, Roebling:
The brilliance and spontaneity of Mozart, the patience
                              of a pyramid,

And requires all these of the painter who at twenty-five
Hardly suspects that in six years he will no longer be alive!
  —His marvellous little marbles, beads, or molecules
Begin as points which the alchemy's magic transforms
Into diamonds of blossoming radiance, possessing and
                                                    blessing the visual:
For look how the sun shines anew and newly, transfixed
By his passionate obsession with serenity
As he transforms the sunlight into the substance of
pewter, glittering, poised and grave, vivid as butter,
In glowing solidity, changeless, a gift, lifted to
                                                    immortality.

The sunlight, the soaring trees and the Seine
Are as a great net in which Seurat seeks to seize and hold
All living being in a parade and promenade of mild,
                                                    calm happiness:
The river, quivering, silver blue under the light's variety,
Is almost motionless. Most of the Sunday people
Are like flowers, walking, moving toward the river, the
                                  sun, and the river of the sun.
Each one holds some thing or some one, some instrument
Holds, grasps, grips, clutches or somehow touches
Some form of being as if the hand and fist of holding
                                                    and possessing,
Alone and privately and intimately, were the only
                              genuine lock or bond of blessing.

A young man blows his flute, curved by pleasure's
                                                    musical activity,
His back turned upon the Seine, the sunlight, and the
                                                    sunflower day.
A dapper dandy in a top hat gazes idly at the Seine:
The casual delicacy with which he holds his cane
Resembles his tailored elegance.

He sits with well-bred posture, sleek and pressed,
Fixed in his niche: he is his own mustache.
A working man slouches parallel to him, quite
comfortable,
Lounging or lolling, leaning on his elbow, smoking a
meerschaum,
Gazing in solitude, at ease and oblivious or contemptuous
Although he is very near the elegant young gentleman.
Behind him a black hound snuffles the green, blue
ground.
Between them, a wife looks down upon
The knitting in her lap, as in profound
Scrutiny of a difficult book. For her constricted look
Is not in her almost hidden face, but in her holding hands
Which hold the knitted thing as no one holds
Umbrella, kite, sail, flute or parasol.

This is the nervous reality of time and time's fire which
turns
Whatever is into another thing, continually altering
and changing all identity, as time's great fire
burns (aspiring, flying and dying),
So that all things arise and fall, living, leaping and
fading, falling, like flames aspiring, flowering,
flying and dying—
Within the uncontrollable blaze of time and of history:
Hence Seurat seeks within the cave of his gaze and
mind to find
A permanent monument to Sunday's simple delight;
seeks deathless joy through the eyes immortality;
Strives patiently and passionately to surpass the fickle
erratic quality of living reality.

Within this Sunday afternoon upon the Seine
Many pictures exist inside the Sunday scene:

Each of them is a world itself, a world in itself (and as a
        living child links generations, reconciles the estranged
        and aged so that a grandchild is a second birth, and the
            rebirth of the irrational, of those who are forlorn,
                resigned or implacable),
Each little picture links the large and small, grouping
                the big
Objects, connecting them with each little dot, seed or
                black grain
Which are as patterns, a marvellous network and tapestry,
Yet have, as well, the random freshness and radiance
Of the rippling river's sparkle, the frost's astonishing
                systems,
As they appear to morning's waking, a pure, white
                delicate stillness and minuet,
In December, in the morning, white pennants streaked
                upon the windowpane.

He is fanatical: he is at once poet and architect,
Seeking complete evocation in forms as strong as the
                Eiffel Tower,
Subtle and delicate too as one who played a Mozart
                sonata, alone, under the spires of Notre-Dame.
Quick and utterly sensitive, purely real and practical,
Making a mosaic of the little dots into a mural of the
                splendor of order:
Each micro pattern is the dreamed of or imagined
                macrocosmos
In which all things, big and small, in willingness and
                love surrender
To the peace and elation of Sunday light and sunlight's
                pleasure, to the profound measure and order of
                proportion and relation.

He reaches beyond the glistening spontaneity

Of the dazzled Impressionists who follow
The changing light as it ranges, changing, moment by
  moment, arranging and charming and freely bestowing
All freshness and all renewal continually on all that
                                    shows and flows.

Although he is very careful, he is entirely candid.
Although he is wholly impersonal, he has youth's
                        frankness and, such is his candor,
His gaze is unique and thus it is intensely personal:
It is never facile, glib, or mechanical,
His vision is simple: yet it is also ample, complex,
                                    vexed, and profound
In emulation of the fullness of Nature maturing and
        enduring and toiling with the chaos of actuality.

An infinite variety within a simple frame:
Countless variations upon a single theme!
Vibrant with what soft soft luster, what calm joy!
This is the celebration of contemplation,
This is the conversion of experience to pure attention,
Here is the holiness of all the little things
Offered to us, discovered for us, transformed into the
                                    vividest consciousness,
After the shallowness or blindness of experience,
After the blurring, dirtying sooted surfaces which, since
                                    Eden and since birth,
Make all the little things trivial or unseen,
Or tickets quickly torn and thrown away
En route by rail to an ever-receding holiday:
—Here we have stopped, here we have given our hearts
To the real city, the vivid city, the city in which we
                                    dwell
And which we ignore or disregard most of the
                                    luminous day!

127

. . . Time passes: nothing changes, everything stays the
                                  same. Nothing is new
Under the sun. It is also true
That time passes and everything changes, year by year,
                                   day by day,
Hour by hour. Seurat's *Sunday Afternoon along the
                          Seine* has gone away,
Has gone to Chicago: near Lake Michigan,
All of his flowers shine in monumental stillness
                                   fulfilled.
And yet it abides elsewhere and everywhere where
                                   images
Delight the eye and heart, and become the desirable,
                          the admirable, the willed
Icons of purified consciousness. Far and near, close and
                                 far away
Can we not hear, if we but listen to what Flaubert tried
                                 to say,
Beholding a husband, wife and child on just such a day:
Ils sont dans le vrai! They are with the truth, they have
                             found the way
The kingdom of heaven on earth on Sunday summer
                                   day.

Is it not clear and clearer? Can we not also hear
The voice of Kafka, forever sad, in despair's sickness
                              trying to say:
"Flaubert was right: *Ils sont dans le vrai!*
Without forbears, without marriage, without heirs,
Yet with a wild longing for forbears, marriage, and
                                 heirs:
They all stretch out their hands to me: but they are too
                               far away!"